Hello Sailor

D1583900

Previous books by the same author:

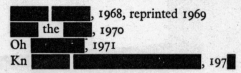

████ ██████, 1968, reprinted 1969
████ the ████, 1970
Oh ███████, 1971
Kn ████ █████████████████, 197█

Eric Idle

Hello Sailor

Futura Publications Limited
A Contact Book

A Contact Book

First published in Great Britain in 1975
by Weidenfeld and Nicolson Limited

First Futura Publications edition 1975
published in association with Weidenfeld
and Nicolson

Copyright © Eric Idle 1975

This book is sold subject to the condition
that it shall not, by way of trade or
otherwise, be lent, re-sold, hired out or
otherwise circulated without the publisher's
prior consent in any form of binding or
cover other than that in which it is
published and without a similar condition
including this condition being imposed on the
subsequent purchaser.

ISBN: 0 8600 7235 5

All characters in this book are completely ▓▓▓▓
fictitious and any resemblance between living persons is
▓▓▓ entirely coincidental.

Printed in Great Britain
by Richard Clay (The Chaucer Press) Ltd,
Bungay, Suffolk

Futura Publications Limited
49 Poland Street, London W1A 2LG

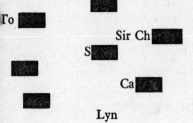

To

Sir Ch

S

Ca

Lyn

Erratum:

page 26, line 31
for
██████ ████ ████ ████ ████ ██████

please read
██████ ████ ████ ████ ████ ██████

Monday

The Prime Minister was very much in love. He sat pinkening slightly in the sauna bath at Number Ten, his loins modestly covered by a large white towel on which was emblazoned 'Hotel Renege, Amsterdam'. He hadn't been so in love since Oxford. His slightly corpulent body glowed with an excess of flesh: he felt healthy and young again. Anything was possible. Soon get the country on its feet. Been a bit restless and shifty till now, still love was a wonderful thing. Next to him on the hot wooden rack the blond boy read *'Figure Weekly'*. His towel – stolen from the same hotel – was underneath his buttocks. There was nothing between him and the admiring gaze of the Prime Minister as he flicked the page and inwardly aspired to the greased perfection of the muscle men. Now there was a real man's man. The Prime Minister was a man's man too.

Monday was M-Day. That's what they'd all been saying for weeks. M-Day. Metrification Day. A giant stride into the technological future. From today forth there would be (legally an'all) only ten inches in the British foot, instead of twelve. 'Piss!' thought Jonathan Beech. It was a depressing thought to wake up of a morning and find your cock was one inch smaller. Even if it was in name alone. To help our exports the papers had said. To make things easier for the businessman dealing with the Continent. He couldn't for the life of him see how shortening the inches in his penis helped the British businessman. Still, international trade's a funny business. He spoke into the sleeping ear next to him.

'D'you know my cock's smaller?'

'Than whose?' asked a sleepy voice.

The Foreign Secretary was dead. Undeniably deceased, he sat stiffly at his desk in the big, wide office. He'd been dead four months now. Passing away inconsiderately at the height of an international crisis, the Cabinet had deemed it best to leave him be lest the announcement of his passing-on cause a loss of confidence in British policy with all the inherent dangers of a run on the pound. So economics kept him alive after politics had killed him. He remained Foreign Secretary. A tasteful taxidermist from Edgware, bribed to secrecy, had made a fine job of him without fuss or smell. In fact the Foreign Secretary had always had a rather moribund look which helped the job considerably. Barrington was his name. Admiral Barrington he liked to be called. He'd never actually been in the navy

2

but he'd always been fond of sailors. 'The Admiral' everybody called him – you don't argue with money. Mrs Bingham was sweeping up round him even now as his unblinking eyes stared down at yesterday's headlines.

'Morning Admiral. Been working late? Ah well don't overdo it. It's not worth it. It kills you.' She cheerfully spoke truer than she knew and left rattling her buckets. In front of him 'The *Sunday Games'* thundered disapprovingly at bomb outrages. Folded neatly inside, its colour supplement showed with diagrams how the petrol bomb was manufactured.

At his desk the Admiral sat, a tribute to modern taxidermy. Many have been advised, recommended and told, yet he was the first Foreign Minister actually to *get* stuffed.

Jim Sickert had left this earth two and a half days before. However he was still very much alive. He lay on his mattress and looked out of the cabin window at the blackness of space and tried not to think about what was bugging him: Andy Scheist and Richard Grabowsky were going to the moon but he wasn't. Simple as that. Fine, he was going 99.9 per cent of the way to the moon, but he wasn't going to step on to the surface. And they were. He hadn't been chosen. Good enough to pilot the fucking pair of them there, pick them up afterwards and do just about everything short of wipe their arses back and forth but no, not actually step out onto the moon. It was enough to make you cry. Hell, he had no quarrel with the method of selection – just the result. They'd been marched to the Mission Control Centre and the MSC leader had made the first stage decision on who would get the EVA from the lunar module and who would remain at the controls of the mother ship *Pelican*. First the Controller looked carefully at their records and then looked carefully at them, and then he spoke: 'Dip dip, dip, my little ship, sails on the o-cean, you are *it*.' Jim Sickert was *it*.

He bet it'd been fixed. Wouldn't be hard to fix something like that. They had computers to help. Besides Richard Grabowsky was Jewish. The first Jewish astronaut. What a help he'd been on the launch: 'All systems go already.' What kind of bloody dialogue was that? My God they'll be sending a Negro up next. And then, who knows, even a woman. Jesus, think of that. He paused. A light blinked. Christ they were on television again. He reached for the book in front of him and started to read soberly aloud. 'In the beginning was the Word. And the Word was with God. And the Word was God.' He knew what the Word was alright. One of these days he might just slip it in for the viewing millions.

One hundred and fifty thousand miles away in Houston Mrs Sickert smiled tenderly. 'That's your Daddy, Neil. Say hello to your Daddy.'

'Lo Daddy.'

The man from *Time* magazine wrote 'Lo Daddy' in his book.

Jim Sickert was reading the Bible at 25,000 miles an hour as they rapidly closed with the moon. Jim Sickert was pissed off.

Jonathan looked at the sleeping armpit beside him and thought about metrification. His eyes noted a hint of five o'clock shadow in that armpit, nevertheless his mind felt better about the missing inch. It hadn't seemed to make much difference after all. A theoretical inch it might have been yet it still had to stand up to test conditions and it had, successfully and with no complaint. He reached up and pulled the number three from a ring-leaved holder. The number four stared down at him. Four of them. So far so good. Perhaps I should explain. It is Jonathan's ambition to fuck all the daughters of the Cabinet. This has been attempted before but never successfully executed. The closest anybody came – if you'll pardon the expression – was in the twenties when a Cambridge undergraduate came very close with a nine out of a Cabinet of eighteen, though there were only ten daughters of penetrable age. He had been very close but the daughter of the Minister of Fuel and Power at that time had steadfastly refused to crack. It seems bad luck on the undergraduate (Herrington his name) but she was later to become a famous lesbian. Indeed had he delayed his attempt just two years that minister was ruined and replaced in the Cabinet by a golf fanatic whose daughter was so famous for it she was called 'The British Open'. Still, that was part of the appeal, the timing. Jonathan lived in daily dread of a reshuffle. You've got to have one complete Cabinet to qualify, and these days that doesn't last long. He'd started off with the daughter of the Min. of Ag. and Fish but he no longer counted her. Her father was not in the Cabinet and not likely to be, still this minister's daughter got him hooked on the game. His first one to count was the daughter of the Minister for Scotland, a red-haired girl who was incredibly shy and went like the clappers, all through a hunt ball in Gloucestershire. He'd watched the dawn come up over her ginger puss and they'd both been asked to leave, by a man in a pink hunting coat who found them going down on each other and wasn't quite sure what they were doing.

His second was the Ministry of Transport, appropriately enough in the back of a car – her red mini van which she'd been given for being twenty-one. Quite an achievement the way she drove it.

'Do you mind?' he had asked her.

'Heavens no, Daddy's always doing it.'

He had decided not to chase the remark, prefering bad grammar to the more obvious implication that the Minister of Transport was in the habit of leaping into bed with his daughter. Cabinet hunting had its dangerous side too.

His third – the fourteen year old daughter of the Minister of Education, still at school at a London comprehensive – had had him. She had jumped into his bed at a party and refused to leave until (her words) 'he'd given her a good seeing to'. She'd wanted to beat him too, but he was shocked and wouldn't let her.

'You were quite good' she said, rolling herself a spliff. 'But not as good as our maths teacher.'

'He's clever with his angles?' he suggested tetchily.

'Hell no, he's a she.'

He'd thrown her out. Gradualism was his school. He was morally shocked.*

And now Number Four lay asleep beside him – the Ministry of Posts and Telecommunications. She'd been pretty good, several times. Oh, in addition he'd had the daughter of the Minister for Wales, in a tent during an eisteddfod. She'd agreed on the condition he introduced her to the Famous Television Personality he worked for. He rather thought that the Famous Television Personality had had her too. In any case, what a welcome she kept in those hillsides.

So there was the list, and he thought himself very fair for not counting the extra two of non-Cabinet status. Four down. Six to go.

The Under-secretary paced the corridor of Number Ten. 'He'll have to come out of that bloody sauna bath.'

'He said he'll come when he's ready sir.'

'Dammit we've got a bloody country to run' said the Under Secretary. 'There's bloody riots at Cambridge and he's stuck in the sauna bath with his little blond friend.'

'Really sir, I feel you should perhaps. . .'

'Look, go and tell him if he's not out in five minutes I'll tell the Home Secretary about his friend.'

'I say that's most uncivil of you, Jeffrey' said the

---

* Serve him right. Ed.

Prime Minister, appearing slightly pink in a small yellow towel. There was a very hurt look in the PM's eyes as he entered the room. He looked at that moment like a little boy of ten.

'I am the Prime Minister and I won't have you threatening me. Do you hear me?'

'Yes. By the way, do you know they're starting to call you the Queen of Sheba?'

'Where?'

'In the office.'

'Sticks and stones.'

'Not at all. As Prime Minister, words are the only things that can hurt you.'

'Oh don't lecture me, Jeffrey.'

'All right, but you'll have to sign these for me now. I've got to take them to the Palace for bloody Madam to sign before midnight.'

'Please don't call Her Majesty that, Jeffrey. How is she?'

'Pestering. She wants to know why you won't go near her.'

'Really Jeffrey I am extremely busy. I hope you told Her Majesty that.'

'Yes, I lied for you. Now please sign these.'

'Your bluntness, Jeffrey, while wholly admirable does wear quickly. What are these?'

'Only Bills.'

'Which ones?'

'Oh the Protest Bill and some others about the Unions.'

'When were they decided?'

'At the Cabinet Meeting. Honestly don't you ever

listen? From midnight it will be illegal to protest about any legally passed bill.'

'But my dear Jeffrey, that covers almost everything.'

'Yes, clever isn't it? It was the Home Secretary's idea.'

'I say, isn't that rather, well,' the Prime Minister lowered his voice, 'undemocratic?'

Jeffrey widened his eyes. 'Law and order, Prime Minister. Law and order. You cannot safeguard democracy and exercise it at the same time. We simply had to choose. And we chose, quite naturally, to defend democracy rather than see it attacked by people who don't care tuppence for it, and who would abuse it, given half a chance to use it.'

'I don't understand all this, Jeffrey.'

'Honestly how did you ever get to be Prime Minister?'

'Don't be beastly, Jeffrey. Its not my fault. They elected me. I didn't want to come here.'

'You were leader of the Party.'

'But I never for a moment suspected we would win, otherwise I wouldn't have accepted. I thought I was just going to be interim leader, thrown over with a peerage when the right man arrived, instead I find I'm Prime Minister. Its too awful really.'

'Well you're stuck with it so you might as well make the best of it.'

'Why did they choose me anyway? Not because of me – no, they thought they'd have a batchelor for a change. A batchelor gay am I. Ha! Change the image of the Party.'

'If only they knew.'

'Please leave Bobo out of this. Incidentally I hope you've booked him with me to Constantinople.'

'Istanbul.'

'What?'

'Not Constantinople. Istanbul. They changed it – in the twenties. You're worse than the Foreign Secretary.'

'How is the Foreign Secretary?'

'Stiff as a poker but nobody's noticed. They took him to a dinner the other night.'

'Good God, he didn't speak?'

'No, but I got one of our chaps to make him applaud. Came out rather well. Matter of fact I'm looking for a discreet ventriloquist. He hasn't made a speech since July and that's a long time even for one of our Foreign Secretaries.'

'Well what are we going to do with him? People are bound to find out, then there'll be a to-do and my reputation will be ruined.'

'Even the press know he's dead.'

'Why don't they print it?'

'Who'd believe them?'

'That's clever.'

'We haven't even put a D-Notice on them. They think they're making a responsible collective moral decision not to publish for the sake of the nation's morale.'

'Well really. . .'

'I know. Still a few CBEs on bloody Madam's birthday wouldn't go adrift.'

'Jeffrey, I really must insist that you stop calling her bloody Madam.'

'Why? She likes it.'

'How odd. What's she like?'

The Under-Secretary raised his eyes to the absent heavens. 'Prime Minister, you can go and see her any time you like. You're supposed to, you know.'

'Oh, I don't much care for women.'

The Vice-President of the United States of America stood to attention stark naked in the shower whilst it played The Stars and Stripes. Vice-President Bugle was extremely proud of his patriotic stereo shower attachment. He'd had it fitted as a present to himself when he'd been chosen as Veep. Been rather a surprise that – to him and everybody – but somebody had to be Veep and somebody objected to everybody else so they'd chosen him. Nobody had objected when his name came up. In fact everybody laughed. Still no one *had* objected and so he had become Vice-President, and now he was only a heart's beat away from the Presidency – assuming that the President had a heart.

Vice-President Bugle pulled the cord and simultaneously the cold water stopped falling on his hairy shoulders and the Armfield Military Academy ceased playing The Stars and Stripes in stereo. He stepped out, cleansed and patriotic.

The red phone rang. The President. Not even pausing for a towel he answered it. The heavy echo told him that the President was phoning from the lavatory again. A great problem were the President's bowels. They steadfastly refused to behave in an all-American way.

So far their intractability had directly escalated the war in South-East Asia and caused severe cut-backs in the Medicare Program. He vented his constipated fury on South-East Asia – that was where his blockage was released. It had got so bad that only a couple of months ago the Commander-in-Chief had ordered American troops into Thailand. He had however, agreed to compromise after a late bowel movement. American troops would – and did – go in but they would be disguised as Cambodians. A master stroke this. That night American troops had donned black pyjamas and opened many thousands of tins of Tin-Tan, a greenish-yellow make-up. So disguised, they had set out to attack the forest. Three months later they were still looking for Communists. They had been bombed several times by the USAF and strafed by their own helicopters in their distinctive black pyjamas and yellow faces but despite digging up several caches of arms specially buried for them by the CIA whilst the newsreels were fortunately on hand, there was a persistent rumour that if they did not soon find a Communist, General Atkinson would go back to General Motors.

This was as nothing however to the president at this time. He was sitting happily in the presidential bathroom with his trousers round his ankles explaining to Bugle his new idea.

'You're gonna like this Norman. We are going to extend the war in South-East Asia. Guess where to?'

'China?'

'No, Norman. We are going to extend the war in South-East Asia to Europe.'

'Europe?'

'That's it. You said it. Wow! D-Day Norman. That's the key.'

'D-Day.'

'D-Day. Yessir. We need another D-Day. Raise morale, get the country behind us. We had no Peace Movements for D-Day. We are going to have us a big sea invasion. In colour.'

'We're going into China.'

'Not China, Norman. Normandy.'

'We're gonna *attack* France?'

'Liberate, Norman. Liberate.'

'Who from?'

'Communists!'

'Listen George, I'm against Communists as much as anybody, hell, more so. . .'

'We're all set at our end. Warner Brothers have put up half the money. . .'

'Warner Brothers? What have they got to do with it?'

'Well, they're half the money. They'll provide the stock and the cutting facilities, shoot it as we go in. They get fifty per cent of the world distribution rights and we just provide the hardware.'

'Oh.'

'Listen, do you know Omar Shariff?'

'I've heard of him of course Mr President.'

'Well he'll be in charge. Its all part of the deal. Warners had to have somebody with box office appeal to be General, so I agreed to that. Oh, and they think they can get Liz Taylor. We start shooting next month. Oh and Norman. . .'

'Yes Mr President?'
'I'm going to be in the film.'

Lady Candida was a groupie. A full time fan of fellatio. Educated, sophisticated, the product of a perfect true-blue background, the daughter of the Chancellor of the Exchequer, heiress, peeress, debutante, paragon of Conservative womanhood she liked nothing more than spending her time on her knees with her mouth full of working-class cock. She was also fond of what is known in cockney circles as 'taking it up the plaster.' In fact almost any orifice, crook or cranny of her raddled nineteen year old body was available for intro or extromission except the most obvious. She was saving that for marriage. Buggered by the gardener at her expensive Welsh public school, her small anus deflowered amongst the flowers, she had since developed a penchant for 'the back door' as she rather tweely called it when requesting service of same. She would make an ideal catch for a Guards Officer.

Unaware of this putative end to her career as a mouth organ she lay curled in a chair, with one leg swinging loosely, speaking to 'Mummy' on the phone. Even as she spoke gazing out into the middle distance through the window her free hand strayed idly towards the zipper on a tight pair of jeans next to her.

'Gosh Mummy that would be super. Really it would. Yes of course I'm behaving myself – oh Mummy you're such a dear.'

Slowly, achingly, her fingers pulled down the zip and disappeared inside.

'Is Daddy frightfully busy? I bet he is. Honestly there's no need for you both to worry. I'm having a frightfully nice time with balls and things. What? Yes, uhm, terribly busy. Oh, this and that. Yes, of course, I take care. Yes really Mummy. Oh hang on. I must go now Mummy, yes I really must – Roger's coming.'

He was.

Halfway along the Brompton Road on his way to Harrods, Jonathan stopped and wrote down a tasteless ad lib for the Famous Television Personality he worked for. A Nun, her habit bulging with large objects bumped into him.

'Fuck,' said the Nun, emptying some of the gifts into a bag, and winking at him.

'Bloody shoplifters' thought Jonathan. Swinging into the Food Hall he collided abruptly with a long-faced thin gentleman wearing a grey overcoat and carnation. The long thin face lengthened and spoke.

'Good Lord, Jonathan what are you doing here?'

'I'm looking for Number Five.'

'I say, what on earth do you mean?'

'Oh nothing. It's difficult to explain. Its a sort of quest I'm on.'

'Sounds frightfully exciting.'

'Mm. It is. You haven't seen the Home Secretary's daughter by any chance?'

15

'My dear chap, I haven't seen a Home Secretary since father threw one out of the House for belching at breakfast. Now he positively hates Home Secretaries – won't have them in the grounds. He sacked one of our gardeners last week for just looking like a Home Secretary. Deuced awkward, him being Speaker and all.'

'Well it's the daughter I'm after. Married, about thirty-eight. Actually I'm not really relishing the prospect, she sounds terribly dull.' And he prodded a melon with the tip of his umbrella. An Attendant bristled.

'Not ripe' said Jonathan pleasantly. 'Hey, what are you doing here anyway Cecil? It's a bit far off your track.'

'I come to bury Caesar.'

'What?'

'I've come to bury my friend.'

'Who?'

'Nigel. Writer chappie. In advertising. Very nice. You'd like him. Went and killed himself chasing a fox. Bloody silly really. Still, we caught the fox. Anyway the thing is he had this whim about being buried in Harrods – so I've brought him.'

'Where is he?'

'Here actually.' Cecil held up a small ornamental casket.

'Is *that* him?'

'Yes. Alas poor Yorick and all that sort of thing.'

'What are you going to do with it?'

'I'm going to scatter him over Harrods.'

'You can't do that.'

'I jolly well can. They wrote me a perfectly beastly

16

letter back when I asked them politely if I might.'

'I'm not surprised.'

'Some silly rot about hygiene and the Public Health Authorities. Well a chap's last request can't be silenced by the regulations of the National Health Service. Nigel was a private patient anyway.'

'But you can't scatter him here, now.'

'Just watch me. I'm going to start off in the Food Hall – leave a bit of him in the plant section and then he was always fond of the gift section so I'll leave just a gnats of him there and then on through kitchenware, hardware, music and so on. Actually I don't think there's very much of him to go round, they're very mean with their ashes at these modern places. You get just a token ash – oh, oh, look out!'

As if some secret Harrodian defences had been tripped, three large impeccably dressed gentlemen were bearing down the Main Food Hall towards them. Swiftly Cecil opened the hideous casket which bravely bore the legend 'London Borough of Hendon', and taking a pinch of rather greyish powder he scattered it grandly with a sweep of the arm. Seeing this the three men increased their pace. Not at all alarmed Cecil turned and made off past the Health Food Store towards the lifts. Open pursuit from the three gentlemen.

'Ashes to ashes' intoned Cecil and, rather irreverantly, 'Bye Nigel', as he shook a little of his late friend into the lift hall.

'Please use the ashtrays provided' said the curt rep tones of the actor/lift attendant as the doors closed. A crowd of pursuers caught up with Jonathan and pushed him into the next lift.

'Follow that lift' said Jonathan to the rather ancient lift attendant. He ignored the remark and tried to remember his lines:

'First floor ladies wear, over the bridge to. . .'

'Shut up' said the Head of Harrod's Defences, eyeing Jonathan suspiciously.

'I am not a party to it' said Jonathan after a while, to no one in particular. 'I am merely an observer.'

At last the doors disgorged them into the upper reaches. It was obvious that here too word had got about. Three or four rather younger gentlemen now gave chase. Occasionally he caught a glimpse of Cecil, careering and skipping along carpeted alleyways, scattering from side to side like a sower of seed. Jonathan wondered vaguely how much of Nigel there was left to go round as he watched Cecil bouncing gleefully through the Pets' Department. (There he seemed not to scatter out of a proper respect for the departed. Nobody, after all, wants their ashes eaten by a pet mongoose, or an unsold lapdog.) But further than the Pets' Department Jonathan did not go – for here he found Number Five.

'Hello, I'm Jonathan' he said. 'You look ever so much younger than your photographs.'

'I am' she said.

As he followed the Home Secretary's daughter into a taxi he saw Cecil being led away. He waved cheerfully at Jonathan.

'All gone,' he said.

'He's a fairy sir,'

'Who's a fairy?'

'The PM, sir. Bent as a hat stand.'

'That's not very funny Splendiman.'

'I know, sir. A faggot at Number Ten. Think of that sir. What a blow for the democratic processes. A fairy. Blimey.'

'Will you stop saying that. Its not funny. Its in extremely bad taste. I've got no time for these stupid office jokes.'

'It's not a joke, sir. He is one of them.'

'Who?'

'The PM, sir. He's queer.'

'Good Lord!'

'He's got a little friend. At it like knives they are sir.'

'But you're supposed to defend him Splendiman.'

'Only from assault sir. I can't stop what's going on in the sauna bath.'

'I don't believe it.'

'It's true sir. We've got a poof Prime Minister.'

'That's in extremely poor taste Splendiman.'

'Sorry sir.'

'If the PM does have a – shall we say –*penchant* . . .'

'Proclivity.'

'*Penchant* for the same sex. . .'

'Little boys sir.'

'Then let us not judge a man too harshly. After all, think of the Greeks.'

'Bloody Onassis isn't bent sir.'

'The Ancient Greeks, Splendiman.'

'He's not young sir, Onassis, but he likes women.'

'I'm much more concerned about Cambridge.'

'Bleedin' students. Always rioting.'

'Reading, rioting and arithmetic.'

'What sir?'

'Nothing Splendiman. Just something for my speech. Should be worth a titter.'

'What do they do? That's what gets me.'

'Come now Splendiman, you must know what chaps get up to.'

'The students, sir? What do they do for the country?'

'What does anybody do for the damn country Splendiman? Its all most unfortunate this Cambridge business. I told the magistrate three months suspended, I even wrote it down for him. But of course he's as blind as a bat. Gave the fellow three years instead. Well I can't blame them rioting.'

'No cause sir.'

'Three years is bloody hard.'

'It's criminal.'

'Exactly.'

'No, what they do sir is criminal. Three years isn't good enough.'

'Precisely what I told the magistrate. Three years isn't good enough. It's not as though its a little mistake. I've accepted the fellow's retirement and he'll only get a knighthood, nothing more. I've seen to that. Dammit we only looked at their files in the first place to see if there was anyone suitable for a job here. We were recruiting not snooping.'

'And now Himself camp as bloody blood island.'

'These are difficult times Splendiman.'

'Bloody difficult sir.'

'The President of the United States? Phoning here? Hold on one second operator.' Jeffrey cupped the receiver with his palm. 'It's the President, Prime Minister. They want to know if you'll accept the call. It's collect.'

'He's never reversed the charges.'

'Fraid so old bean.'

'The very nerve.' He took the receiver from Jeffrey. 'Mr President. Well, hello. This is a priviledge. What's that?'

'Garble garble garble garble.'

'You're kidding.'

'Garble garble. Bargle bargle bargle.'

'No, no, you can't. You're not allowed to. Wait. No, its all right operator we're still talking. Yes I know other people may want the line. Mr President are you still there? Hello? No, not you operator. Hello, Mr President? Listen, we're... No, *we're* paying for this call. Operator will you kindly get off the line!'

The PM held the receiver up. Across the Atlantic came the unmistakeable sound of a lavatory flushing. The PM replaced the receiver.

'What's he want?'

'He wants to take out Cambridge.'

'Take out?'

'Bomb. Destroy.'

'Why?'

'He's got some crazy scheme with Warner Brothers – I didn't entirely understand it. Something to do with protecting his back door, with all this rioting. It's too much for me. Where's Bobo?'

'Mr Prime Minister. . .'

'I know what you are going to say Jeffrey. You're going to be quite right, but just you get on with it for me. Good heavens can't I have five minutes to myself a day without some crisis or another? Its really too bad. Now call a Cabinet Meeting or something. Oh and you'd better alert the Foreign Office, if there's anybody still alive there. Now where *is* Bobo?'

The Cabinet met at two. They sat gravely in the oak-panelled room waiting for the PM. Upstairs his sun-ray lamp pinged. He got up and started to dress.

Downstairs the Home Secretary sat at the head of the table unaware that at this very moment his married daughter was straddling Jonathan in their Mayfair apartment. The Chancellor too was unaware that his daughter's devoted lips were working overtime on the drummer of 'Loud Noise' and the Minister of Posts, slumbering slightly, remained blissfully ignorant that *his* daughter was douching away the last of Jonathan to prepare for the first of the Shadow Minister for Home Affairs. (Yes, that most heinous of Tory female crimes – receiving a Labour member.)

The Minister for Pollution was reading a paperback

wrapped inside the White Paper on ecology. It was obviously exciting him. Reluctantly he closed the book and looked up.

In their different places Jonathan and the Prime Minister entered simultaneously.

'Five!' thought Jonathan.

'Oh bollocks,' thought the PM. But he said 'Good morning, Gentlemen.'

'Good morning' they all said. It was afternoon but you don't argue when you're in the Cabinet.

The PM sat down, glancing at the empty chair beside him. 'You'd better bring Barrington in. It looks better.'

There was a slight commotion as both double doors were thrown open and two men in green baize aprons lurched in carrying the late Foreign Secretary horizontally. The foremost of the two setting down the Minister's stiff feet, kicked him behind the knee into a sitting position. The other man slammed the chair tight to the table, wedging Admiral Barrington's stomach against it. The Foreign Secretary tippled ever so slightly forward and sideways, his eyes staring askew at the corner of the table like a set-down ventriloquist's dummy.

'That'll do' the PM said tetchily.

The Gay Liberation Front was on the march. Rally at 2.30 it had said, and promptly at half-past they trolled off towards Downing Street, five hundred or more marching in a happy but determined way behind a couple of embarrassed constables.

The photographers were there of course and the various televisions, but apart from the media nobody took much notice. Just another protest. Several large banners carried their encapsulated messages to the world: 'Go Gay', 'Bent is Beautiful', and a couple of very rude ones which the cameras tried to miss. Here and there green eyeshadow glinted in the sunshine. and there was a generous smattering of drag.

When they got there Downing Street was of course barricaded. A dozen or so policemen stood sheepishly behind the barricades pretending they weren't there and a further green bus-load tried to look gently unconcerned behind them.

'I hope they don't scratch' said one, and there were nervous police titters.

From behind the barricade Splendiman watched the protest morosely. A queer-basher by nature, he was disturbed by his knowledge and divided in his loyalty. His natural instincts told him to put the boot in – 'Perverts. It was illegal in my day' – and yet his protective instincts swaddled his charge, the Prime Minister. Impaled on his own snobbery and utterly confused, he watched them line up and exercise the Englishman's inalienable right to shout abuse down Downing Street. It fell on the deaf ears of the dead Foreign Secretary. The Cabinet rising hastily were cowering downstairs with sandwiches.

A few yards away some of the Police were beginning to fraternize with the demonstrators, perhaps mistaking them for women – perhaps not. 'Even the Police'

24

thought Splendiman savagely. 'If I had my way. . .' But the crowd were calling for the resignation of the Prime Minister. Suddenly Splendiman found himself laughing.

'Out, out, out!' they shouted.

He stood there rocking uncontrollably as they howled for the PM's head. 'If only they knew. If only they bloody well knew.'

'So we're selling them the tanks.'

'Yes, yes, a fine decision, bravely taken. The PM was most keen on the idea. Loyalty. He likes the thought.'

'That'll cause trouble in Istanbul.'

'Oh bugger the Commonwealth Jeffrey. We are not going to have our policies dictated to us by a lot of natives. Whose Commonwealth is it anyway? These are our kith and kin in South Africa and skin is thicker than water. Besides they need our tanks desperately.'

'What for?'

'Everybody needs tanks. Its a fact of life. And think of our Balance of Payments.'

These were the considered words of the Home Secretary. He was standing with Jeffrey in the first-floor morning room that lay above the now vacated Cabinet Room. Through the window they watched Bobo and the Prime Minister throwing a large beach-ball about.

'Gay, gay, gay . . .' drifted up the road from the barricades.

Unheeding, the Prime Minister played happily, pinkening about his chubby cheeks. He looked as though he was on his school hols. Bobo was.

'I hope he won't miss his plane' grumbled the Home Secretary.

'As long as he's happy' said Jeffrey tolerantly.

'Oh I think he'll manage the Conference extremely well. Once he makes his mind up he's pretty good you know.'

They watched him scampering after the yellow beach-ball.

'They'll give him hell.'

'Yes Jeffrey, I know.' The Home Secretary didn't look too unhappy at the prospect. Jeffrey decided to change the subject.

'And what are we to do about Cambridge?'

'I'm Oxford myself,' said the Home Secretary ruminatively. 'Of course we shan't allow the Americans to kill anybody, you know. They will simply occupy Cambridge for a few days to reassure themselves, and we shall simply let them. It's been agreed.'

'If it gets out there's been collusion it'll ruin the Government. It always does.'

'Not collusion dear boy. We have no alternative. The entire army is in Ireland and even if they weren't, their tanks are all parcelled up for South Africa. The navy's steaming hard for Istanbul and the Conference – show the flag, warn the natives, that sort of thing. And. . .'

'Perhaps we should get them back.'

'Perhaps. And as for the RAF nobody knows where they are.'

'Somebody must know.'

'I don't see why they must. The PM doesn't know. They never ask permission for anything, some of them still think there's a war on.'

'Doesn't anybody know where they are?'

'The Russian Embassy said they'd gone to Cyprus for some training exercises.'

'You asked the Russians?'

'Well? At least, they knew. Frankly I'm up to here with the RAF.'

The Prime Minister kicked the yellow beach ball into the bushes. They watched him skip happily after it.

'We're all queers together . . . And jolly good company' sang the crowd distantly.

'Isn't that the Eton Boating Song?' said the Home Secretary.

'Sort of' Jeffrey said. 'Incidentally, there's a rumour going about that the army is behind the bank robberies.'

'Oh come now, really, this is the twentieth century.'

'Maybe, but it *was* you who suggested that bits of the army should be sold off to private enterprise.'

'Only the more profitable bits Jeffrey. You will find that above all I am a most practical man.'

Bobo was now being chased about the garden by the Prime Minister.

'Bent as – a row of pink tents' sang the crowd.

The Home Secretary's brow furrowed slightly. 'Jeffrey.'

'Yes, Home Secretary.'

'Jeffrey, the Prime Minister . . .'

'Yes, Home Sectretary.'

'Well he isn't . . . he isn't just a little bit . . . well, he's not just an ounce . . . *queer?*'

'Just a little bit Home Secretary.'

'Ah.'

There was a long silence. In the garden the PM panted after Bobo.

The Home Secretary's eyes moistened slightly. 'Jeffrey, shall I let you into a secret?'

'What's that?'

'I'm not really the Home Secretary.'

'No?'

'No. Underneath...' he lowered his voice to a whisper '...underneath I'm really Captain Marvellous.' He put his finger to his lips. 'Sh! Don't say anything.'

Jeffrey said nothing. Silently Captain Marvellous left the room in the clothes of the Home Secretary. Turning at the door he winked at Jeffrey. 'Sh. We'll pull through.' Then he left.

Jeffrey looked at the Prime Minister. He had caught Bobo and they were both tugging at the beach-ball.

'They're all bloody mad' said Jeffrey.

'We shall overcome' sang the crowd, optimistically.

CODED TELEX. HM ADMIRALTY
OFFICE DATED MONDAY 1630. MESSAGE
TO HOME FLEET HEADING
ISTANBULWARDS. STOP MOST SECRET
MESSAGE READS STOP. STOP.
WHOLEFLEET RETURN
ENGLANDWARDS MOST
IMMEDIATELY. URGENT STOP.

Back at Captain Marvellous' apartment Jonathan had finished with the Home Secretary's daughter. Five was in the bag. A splendid lady she was, but time was pressing.

'Hey, where do you think you're off to?'

'Er, I've got to go.'

'Not so fast. I haven't finished with you young man.'

She certainly hadn't.

'Splendiman, I have arranged for you to have an assistant in Istanbul.'

'Thank you sir. Pretty dangerous place apparently – full of foreigners.'

'Er yes. I only hope he'll be able to help you.'

'Doubtless sir, doubtless. We must be vigilant of the Prime Minister's person sir.'

'We certainly must', said Jeffrey, 'and that's why I've chosen the right man for the job.'

'I'm amenable to working alongside of whomsoever sir' Splendiman assured him.

'Splendid man' said Jeffrey.

They were both embarrassed at the echo of his name.

'Well er keep your eye on him Splendiman and I want the PM at the airport at ten thirty sharp.'

'I shall move heaven and earth sir to ensure that he shall not arrive in retard.'

'Splen . . . good chap' said Jeffrey.

Nevertheless he was in retard at the airport. And

Splendiman as he would no doubt put it 'incurred the displeasure of his superior's wrath.' Jeffrey in fact was extremely cross. He'd arranged a late flight so they'd get the minimum of press and now the timing was all to cock. Moreover since they were economizing so much he'd booked the PM on a charter flight and the other passengers, a university tour, were getting extremely testy at the delay.

'Send them down some drinks . . . no wait. Belpitt.'

'Sir.'

'Pop across to the Customs and see if they can let you have an ounce of hash. Tell them its for the PM's flight. That should keep them quiet.'

'Sir.'

'Now then Splendiman.'

'I'm sorry sir, its not my fault. He went to a party.'

'Where on earth at, Splendiman?'

'Ampstead.'

'Hampstead?'

'Yes sir. On the Heath. Those queer chappies. . .'

'Splendiman!'

'Yes sir. The Gay Liberation Front were celebrating sir.'

'Good Lord! Was he recognized?'

'No sir, they were all at it. I may say sir I was very lucky to find him. Fortunately there were one or two constabulary present – and they assisted.'

'I hope you warned them to be discreet.'

'Oh yes sir. I've got them over a barrel sir. You see they weren't on duty.'

Jeffrey raised an eyebrow. Sometimes it seemed as if minority groups were gaining ground. A Securicor van drew up and two uniformed guards started to unload a large trunk.

'Ah here's the Foreign Secretary now' said Jeffrey. 'As soon as he's unpacked I want him in the VIP lounge for some photographs with the PM. Our photographer. Keep the press away as far as possible. Oh Splendiman...'

'Sir.'

'Your assistant will be travelling with you. I hope you'll get on.'

'I'm sure I shall.'

'Uhm, well he's over there so you might as well come and meet him.'

A brown trenchcoat with its back towards them successfully concealed its occupant – Special Branch uniform. As they drew closer the figure turned, revealing an unmistakable shock of blond hair and a fresh young face.

'I believe you know Bobo, Splendiman?'

Splendiman choked.

'He'll be assisting you on the trip, if anybody asks.'

Splendiman had an instant nightmare vision of fairies at the bottom of all gardens everywhere.

'How do you do' he muttered.

'Hello luv' said Bobo.

Tuesday

Jonathan woke up alone. Behind him, on the wall, the number five. The half-marker. Christ, she should count double. He'd escaped after ten o'clock only because the House had risen early and her husband, Colonel Cahn-Waters, MP for mid-Sussex, could be expected home as soon as they closed the bars. Mrs Cahn-Waters, nee Miss Home Secretary, was making up for a month in the country and a sitting member for a husband, and she'd exhausted Jonathan.

He had tiptoed from her bedroom only to find the Home Secretary reading in the lounge. There was no other way out.

'Goodnight' he had called cheerfully, letting himself out.

'Goodnight Batman' had said the Home Secretary, not looking up from his . . . *was* it ? . . . a comic?

And now as the sun reluctantly filtered into his basement flat he contemplated his new politics of ecstasy and considered his article for *'Cym'*, an obscene Welsh magazine. Occasionally he dropped them the odd 'thing,' but this would be something different: the full history of his particular brand of phallus-politics, to be tentatively called 'The turn of the screw'. Better wait till after Number ten, he decided – a record is a record is an article.

Modestly putting his white towelling wrap on to avoid the eager eyes of the New Zealand girls upstairs, he went to the front door for the paper. He chose their *Guardian.*

The front page had a picture of the Prime Minister and the Foreign Secretary at an airport news conference. Someone was leaning watchfully over the foreign Secretary. The talk was of hopes, promises, commitments, obligations, necessities, realities, reluctancies . . . he skipped it. The main story concerned the Royal Divorce. There was a diagram of the route the unhappy couple would take in their separate gilt coaches: first to the Abbey and then to the House of Lords for the final dissolution – an AA route from the sublime to the ridiculous. Already the bunting was up and large crowds were expected to line the streets. Very popular is royalty. A Mrs Betty Sutton was going to camp out overnight to secure a good view of the procession. 'I shall be happy if I just see their miserable faces, bless 'em' she was quoted as saying.

The *Guardian* was by no means sure whether the royal divorce would proceed as smoothly as expected. There were several cross-petitions to hear, the most damaging suggestion being that the Royal Princess had been a little too fond of Black Rod. The *Guardian* hoped that the world would be spared these unsavoury details – a hope that the world itself did not share, since thousands were already about the streets, full television coverage was planned and live broadcasting had already started on radio. Their Lordships were queuing hard to secure their seats in the Upper Chamber, obliged to break their custom of non-attendance in the interests of the nation. The nation was indeed interested. If there's one thing better than a public scandal its a Royal Scandal, and for once it wasn't just in the French newspapers. No, this was for everybody. Why, even a Guardsman had been called to give evidence – against the Royal Husband. Jonathan chuckled. Number Six should be easy to locate today of all days, for who would stray far from Westminster?

On the inside pages he found a story about Cecil. 'Arrested in famous Knightsbridge store' said the headline. Somehow convinced that Cecil was a junkie the Police had diligently tested Nigel's ashes for drugs. To their disappointment they found only Nigel. Irritated, they had tried to charge Cecil with being in possession of an offensive body. There was however some legal doubt as to whether ashes actually constituted a body and so to avoid expensive litigation they had simply kicked him a little and charged him with assaulting a police officer.

Cecil had wisely accepted the ten pound fine and indeed had managed to slightly embarrass the police by fulsomely apologising in court to the officer who had kicked him. The unfortunate man, trapped for five minutes while Cecil humbly and nauseatingly apologised from the dock, blushed to his boots. Even the magistrate had noticed and testily wished the police wouldn't clutter the courts with these minor misdemeanours.

At the bottom of the third page Jonathan found a three line snippet.

> Britain's giant prototype supersonic Jumbo, *White Elephant* broke some glass in a Coventry church during flight trials yesterday.

In fact the published story was less than honest. The Coventry church was not a church, so much as *the* Cathedral, and the 'pane' of glass was the entire west wall – sixty feet by thirty feet of finest hand-cut glass totally shattered by the passage of the plane.

The Dean surveyed the jagged ruins as the wicked midland wind whistled in and flapped at the Sutherland.

'Piss the bastards' said the Dean.

'Worse than the Blitz' said Prebendary Morris.

'Each time we get the damn Cathedral up, bloody aircraft knock it down,' said the Dean.

'Per ardua ad astra.'

'We'll have to build the third bugger underground.' said the Dean.

The *White Elephant,* Prototype 2, snug in a hanger near Bristol, was of course unaware of the storm it had created. In France its twin, *'L'Elephant Blanc'* had already caused moderately severe damage to Rheims Cathedral. But the French are a religious nation, and much less worried about their clerical buildings, while the English, thoroughly un-Christian, will go spare at the thought of damaging churches, so the Coventry story was not so much hushed up as changed. The Dean was promised a bishopric, the Bishop was promised an archbishopric, the Archbishop was offered money. The press were easily persuaded to soft-soap the story, as critical sales to America were involved, but actually no *White Elphant* had been sold. Not to no-one. Nowhere. For a start the cost would make an elephant blanche – sixteen million pounds for each – and this was cheap compared to the Anglo French development costs. In August there had been a supreme moment in the history of international cooperation, when the English fuselage had finally come face to face with the French – yes friends – fuselage. Nobody had made the tailplane.

The Minister of Technology, an Oxford classicist, had stepped forward with a speech about the white-hot heat of the technical revolution, and the band had pluckily struck up a medley of Rule Britannia and the Marseillaise but, when the wraps were lifted to reveal the world's first double-barrelled tail-less aeroplane, the splendour had gone out of the occasion and they broke the cameras of the press to be on the safe side.

So the *White Elephant* had progressed from fiasco to worseco. The French Aviation Minister committed suicide shortly afterwards, but as much for some photographs of him and a French actor as for anything else, and as for Britain, well there was an independent tribunal as there always will be, but it was composed of the Prime Minister's brother-in-law, the headmaster of Harrow and a friend of the Royal Family, and its findings took two years to find, and were too dull to publish and added another ten thousand pounds to the cost of the fastest, most expensive, unsaleable, twin-barrelled noise in the world.

Back in South-East Asia, General Atkinson was becoming desperate. Three months and not a single Communist encountered. That was just like the Communists – lousy stinking bastards – no wonder they should be killed. Never even turned up for a fight. And thus frustrated by a lack of enemy he had resorted to the American alternative: he had bought some – quite cheaply, actually. Not real Communists, but hell you'd never tell the difference. They'd toured the most miserable refugee camps (itself no small task) making tempting offers as they went and finally they'd scraped together what they needed most – fifty men. Fifty miserable men who for various agreed sums of money had consented to play the enemy. Uncle Sam hadn't skimped on their mission either. Each man in addition to receiving a large sum of money in cash and a guarantee of a further large sum for his family in the certain event of his decease, had been given a fully automatic weapon, plentiful live ammunition ('We are not going to cheat on this thing' said General Atkinson), supplies for twenty days and a swift political education. In order to ensure complete authenticity, the CIA had provided a five day course in Communism, with CIA men lecturing the chosen fifty on the failure of the profit motive, the evils of capitalism, the spiritual power of the commune, and the strength, bravery and wisdom of Asian freedom fighters. And so, fully equipped mentally and spiritually, to tackle the

American army – itself disguised as Cambodians –these fifty were ferried into the jungle at 06.00 hours to a point called Glade 6; and there they were left.

General Atkinson, mindful of his youth and the fairness of child's play, counted one hundred with his back turned and then screamed 'Attack, attack, attack.' The entire American force moved towards Glade 6.

```
CODED TELEX. BRITISH EMBASSY.
ISTANBUL DATED TUESDAY )(/)0930
MESSAGE TO HOME FLEET. OFF
GIBWARDS. HEADING BRITAINWARDS.
STOP. MOST SECRET STOP URGENT
YOU      ATTEND      CONFERENCEWARDS
STOP
PROCEED INSTANBUL IMMEDIATELY
STOP PRIME MINISTER REPEAT PRIME
MINISTER.
```

'You've turned the fleet.'

'Yes, Jeffrey dear boy. It was such a lovely morning and the harbour here looked so beautiful and I thought the navy would be such a pretty sight for the Conference, such an elegant reminder of our potency, what?'

'Yes Prime Minister but . . . hello? Hello PM?'

'Still here dear boy. The Constantinople telephone service is erratic but efficient in its way.'

'Istanbul.'

'What?'

'Nothing. Listen the Cabinet are very worried about Cambridge.'

'Oh hang the Cabinet.'

'Even the Admiralty's going spare. And we still can't find the RAF.'

'They're in Cyprus.'

'How do you know?'

'Everybody here says so.'

'Well please can you get one of our chaps to confirm it in writing. There's a lot of jealousy here from the army. They want their tanks back – and this RAF business hasn't helped any.'

'Jeffrey, those tanks are our free and inalienable right to trade with whomsoever we wish. Just remember Jeffrey they are not tanks but bridges. Please tell the army so.'

'Not tanks, bridges.'

'Quite right dear boy. And do stop sounding so piqued. Its glorious here, you really should come over.'

'Thanks, I'll probably have to. How was your flight?'

'Oh splendid. Those young people were extremely jolly. Very friendly. First class.'

'So they should have been. We owe the Customs a tenner at current market prices.'

'They gave me an extremely nice Turkish cigarette.'

'What?'

'We all got on swimmingly. Really Jeffrey you should have been there. You'll never guess but a nice *girl* came and sat in my lap.'

'Prime Minister. . .'

'Now don't worry Jeffrey, its quite alright. They were sensible students from Cambridge. . .'

Jeffrey swallowed hard.

'You should have seen Bobo's face when this girl took. . .'

'Did you tell them anything?' Jeffrey had gone quite pale.

'About Bobo?'

'Sod Bobo.'

'Jeffrey!'

'About Cambridge. Did you tell them anything about Cambridge?'

'What about it?'

'About the Americans.'

'Oh that, I don't suppose so.'

'Did you?'

'They were extremely friendly Jeffrey.'

'Did you tell them?'

'I don't know. I like students Jeffrey', said the Prime Minister petulantly, 'and I don't like Americans.'

Jeffrey was sweating. Somewhere in his head he could hear a bomb ticking. The PM was still talking.

'. . . Do you know Jeffrey, they didn't believe I was Prime Minister.'

'Really?' said Jeffrey. The ticking had faded.

'No, they thought I was joking.'

'How funny' said Jeffrey, suddenly light-headed. 'Whatever could have made them think that?'

'What's that?' The PM had detected his sarcasm.

'How is your hotel?' said Jeffrey.

'Beastly. I thought you were going to book Bobo in.'

'I did Prime Minister.'

'Not with me.'

'We have to observe the proprieties, Prime Minister. Even in Istanbul.'

'But he's sharing a room with Splendiman.'

'Yes?'

'Then why can't he share a room with me?'

'Because they aren't ...' Jeffrey stopped hurriedly.
There was a pause.

'No', said the Prime Minister, 'and they better
hadn't.' Click.

The American voice on the radio crackled. 'In Istanbul
the British Prime Minister and the Foreign Secretary
are attending the full opening session of the Commonwealth Conference. They're expected to have a
rough time in the talks because of their decision to sell
tanks to South Africa. In London thousands are
already lining the streets for the Royal Divorce which
is being beamed by satellite to most of the over-
developed countries.

'Basketball. The Philadelphia Sox beat the Boston
Crabs by fifty-seven baskets to fifty-three last night to
give them an overall lead in the national table. Well, I
guess that's just about all the world news for today
Jim.'

PIP: 'Roger.'

MISSION CONTROL: 'The astronauts are now in moon
orbit. The separation phase has taken place sucessfully
and Frank Swineheart has just finished reading the
news to Jim Sickert. Sickert in the mother ship is acting
as a relay signal to the LEM, *Phoenix*. Scheist and
Grabowsky report all is go.'

P I P : 'Best wishes here from the President for Andy and Richard, Jim.'

P I P : 'O K I'll relay that to them.' No best wishes for Jim he thought. He waited two minutes. Did nothing.

P I P : 'They say to thank the President.' (Fuck them, thought Jim, meanly un-American.)

Jim Sickert's wife heard her husband's voice coming from the television. The *Time* magazine reporter's notebook lay on the chair beside her bed where the *Time* magazine reporter lay on top of her. She had her fingers crossed for Jim.

'Good luck Jim', she thought, but 'Yes, yes' she said to the reporter as his thighs worked deliciously on her. He wasn't writing down every reaction of the astronaut's wife.

P I P : 'This is Houston, *Pelican.*'

P I P : 'Go ahead Houston.'

P I P : 'Two minutes till loss of signal.'

P I P : 'Roger. Go condition green.'

Jim Sickert prepared for the seventh time to go behind the moon. But this one was different – this was the first time he went alone. *Phoenix* had separated and was in low orbit preparatory to touchdown. He would now be by himself for a couple of days.

P I P : 'One minute till loss of signal.'

P I P : 'See you on the other side.'

One minute later Jim Sickert went into the darkness behind the back of the moon where his wife already lay.

'Uhm' said Mrs Sickert, as she reported loss of signal.

Istanbul – which the Prime Minister from schoolboy habit persisted in calling Constantinople – lies between the Black Sea and the Sea of Marmara. The Commonwealth Conference just starting was therefore held within cooee of Gallipoli – a poignant if unwelcome reminder of British fallibility. For geographers, Gallipoli is to the left of Istanbul at the bottom of the left hand corner of the Sea of Marmara, which is itself joined to the Aegean by a narrow strip of water called the Dardanelles (named after a music hall joke). The whole area was the scene of some startling British incompetence of which the fleet would not be unaware, should it ever manage to stop passing Gibraltar and actually go somewhere.

Several rounds of talks at lower than ministerial level had been held in successive capitals, but Istanbul had been selected for the final as a neutral ground. There's a lot of money in conferences, as hoteliers anywhere will tell you and so the Turks had readily agreed to play host. They'd installed the British Prime Minister in fine splendour at the Gallipoli Hotel, where he rubbed shoulders with some of the finest shoulders in Europe. Drinks were constantly served should he so require, in the comfort of the Lawrence of Arabia Cockail Lounge. Here he could relax in comfortable surroundings and gaze at the walls hung with photographs of Peter O'Toole, (a failure to differentiate between fact and fantasy which was the keynote of the week).

Through the panoramic window he could see the sparkling blue bay and beyond that the Inner Harbour where the British aircraft carrier *'Triumphant'* lay magnificently at anchor, the epitome of all the finest British maritime traditions – a tall proud ship, ready, willing and able to sail wherever troubled waters ran deep.

In fact she was stuck. Couldn't move. Rammed hard against a sandbank for five years, where she had remained immobile, victim of a spare parts go-slow in a Midlands factory, forever crippled, the most beautifully painted pile of scrap iron in the East. Offically she was still afloat; it said so in Lloyds Register. But the crew had taken odd jobs ashore and the officers used her only for cocktails and gala dances, and spent their time bungalowing themselves to death in the hills nearby.

The ordinary sailors in fact had started a car-hire firm – 'Triumphant Cabs' – a tribute to British thieving, created out of almost nothing but the millions of parts available from the late ship. From this had grown the most profitable sideline the navy had ever run – the Hotel Triumphant. Within four years it had established its reputation world wide. It was the biggest baroque brothel in the world. It catered for tastes people had never tasted let alone catered for. It was the pride and joy of the navy. It had been hired for the conference.

The Hilton of whore houses, it had two advantages for a conference. Firstly, delegates could get 'relief' at any time without having to leave the building, and secondly, a small crowd was always on hand for the news-reels. Actually they were not a crowd but a queue. Still, they came in handy for the cameras when

Heads of State rolled up and the telly audience remained blissfully unaware that the 'large crowds who gathered to welcome the Commonwealth Ministers' were really an Istanbul brothel queue. In any case, they looked quite excited.

Inside, an ornate gilt hall, mirror-lined and voluminous, was a perfect setting for the Conference. Each wall contained expensive two-way glass, electronically controlled, so that at the touch of a button a casual visitor standing in the centre of the room could be instantly plunged into a moving vision of flesh on all sides: flesh against flesh; flesh against anything; anything against flesh. The hundreds of smaller rooms that lay behind the mirrored hall could thus be instantly revealed. It was a work of genius, the product of centuries of maritime experience, and it was run by Seaman Beal.

Seaman Beal was of that breed of stocky little stewards who run all the graft on British Rail. At the outset he decreed there should be no indecorous behaviour in the main hall during the Conference – no nudity, no soliciting, no nothing. If the delegates wanted it, they knew where to get it, but they couldn't have it in the hall. And there was only one small cockup. On the first day – in error so they swear – the official opening document in its bright pink folio was passed around the table for all to sign. Inside they found a black and white close up picture of an utterly naked lady of voluminous parts, triumphantly holding between her legs two British sailors, waving flags of all nations. This picture caused a growing smile around the room as it went, until it reached the British camp.

Here the Truce of Noman lost fifteen dollars in a bet, for the Foreign Secretary never blinked an eye (how could he?) and the British Prime Minister was so far away that he initialled the lady's buttocks. So she too was ratified, while the PM thought only of Bobo.

Meanwhile miles away in misunderstood Wales, cocooned on a dock in Swansea, stood the 250 Centurian Tanks ordered by South Africa for external defence only.

Here was the crux of the conference. For the British it wasn't a moral issue: it was a simple hardware sale, cash down, no problems. So naturally they were bound to be annoyed when a bunch of African leaders suggested it was an immoral and indeed politically naive act. Now, no British government is fond of being called naive, especially by a native, and particularly by a whole roomful of emergent nationals who might be jolly decent chaps in the privacy of their own huts but who simply didn't have the mental equipment to deal with the sophisticated world of international business. African states and African statesmen were there to be visited and photographed by British royalty. This entitled them to give Britain all produce and harvests at specially reduced rates, and to be very grateful for it. Their leaders could if they liked send their children to be buggered at Eton and insulted at Sandhurst, before being shipped home as undesirables, but it didn't give them the right to criticise the mother country when it came to business, or politics, or sport.

Nevertheless the Tanks had been delayed at Swansea to await the outcome of the Conference, and they faced some formidable opposition.

By far the most splendid opponent was the Truce of Noman. Over six feet four and resplendent in national Nomanese costume, this enormous gentleman was daunting enough for anyone, let alone a rather tubby and, shall we say, effete British Prime Minister. And yet the Truce seemed drawn towards the little PM, patronisingly assisting him at every stage, offering him advice, making jokes for him, opening doors for him and escorting him even into the Gents. Wherever the PM went the Truce was sure to follow, so that Istanbul for the British seemed full of Truces, baring the whitest teeth into the widest smiles. Even when the Conference was at its most acrimonious, delegate after delegate rising and denouncing the British, still the Truce managed to smile towards the isolated British delegation where sat the PM, silent, unlistening and asleep, and the Foreign Secretary, stiff, unlistening and dead. And though he too rose and sadly pointed out the inelegance of their ways, yet he seemed to be a friend and comfort to the British in their hour of need.

For Splendiman the Truce posed insurmountable problems. Far from pleased with Jeffrey for accommodating him with Bobo – 'The Prime Minister's gentleman', as he put it – he was even further irritated by the attentions of 'the big black gentleman' towards the little white PM. All day he cursed Jeffrey softly under his breath while eyeing the Truce suspiciously, watching him come dangerously close to the PM – far too close for a man with a Moorish dagger in his waistband. But what could he, Splendiman, do? Wasn't it bad enough sharing a room with that little blond ponce, 'nursing PM's fancy man,' without the PM himself behaving recklessly in front of foreigners. Little bugger never put on any clothes –waltzed around the room in the altogether as if he weren't there. Oh, some things were hard to take. He were only a wee stub of a boy. It were disgusting. At least he should put a stitch on. And then the bloody phone kept ringing. All night calls came through Splendiman, and several times he'd been disturbed by palace officials anxious to speak to the PM. He'd put them off with a variety of invented excuses and towards dawn had finally managed to ignore the insistent ringing and pretend he was asleep. It was Bobo's voice that really woke him. He was answering the phone.

'Yes love?'

Splendiman could hear the other voice distinctly. There was no mistaking it. It would cut through ice.

'Hello, is that the Prime Minister's suite?'

'It certainly is love' said Bobo indulging in a pun. The female voice was regally persistent. Splendiman struggled to wake up, hoping it was a nightmare.

'Who is this please?' said Bobo.

There was a pause at the other end. 'This is the Queen.'

'Oh yes, love. Snap.'

In London it was raining. A light royal drizzle that dampened the crowds and mushroomed umbrellas all down the Mall. The bunting sagged between lines of loud speakers and dripped on the Pacamacs, wetting newspapers into soggy pulp and filling sandwich tins. Lines of youthful soldiery in ceremonial number ones remained immobile and unflinching in the wet, up since dawn, minds elsewhere, from two days polishing. The crowd good humouredly taunted them from time to time.

'Are they real, Norma?'

'No, they'm waxworks.'

Music was everywhere. From a thousand loudspeakers the voice sang. 'I'm getting married in the morning. . .'

'Ding dong the bells' joined in the crowd.

Cockney cheer was everywhere. It was a truly Royal Occasion. Nearer Westminster small groups of Gay Liberators sold their paper *Self Abuse* to unsuspecting tourists. 'The organ of the Homosexual world' they read – too late to get their money back.

'Dad, look what our Pete's been an' bought.'

You can sell a crowd anything. The lead story in *Self Abuse* claimed a world record daisy chain on Hampstead Heath the night before. Fortunately there was no word of it having been official. Today was quite a day for the Front. One of their number, a guardsman, was actually testifying. What a nail-biting moment for some peers. Just how much would he tell? Yes it would be quite a day.

Nearby, Lady Candida was in bed with the Flu. There were five of them: lead guitar, bass, drums, electric piano and rhythm guitar. She was on the electric pianist at the moment.

'Hurry up', said the rhythm guitarist.

At Number eleven Downing Street, her father the Chancellor was presiding over a meeting of the

Cabinet. Upstairs was her room, where once she'd shocked a Catholic MP into submission by going down on him while he argued against women's rights. He hadn't spoken in the House since – just sat there blank-faced. Puzzled. Downstairs a television set, sound off, showed colour pictures of the Royal Route. There was an atmosphere of gloom.

'It is bad news from Istanbul.'

'Not as bad as it might have been, Michael.'

'No, still, I hope he can handle it.'

They didn't look convinced.

'*Would* they break up the Commonwealth?'

'I doubt it. There'd be hell to pay.'

'Aye, and we'd do the paying.'

The irritating sound of hoovering drifted across the room.

'Sorry' said the Chancellor. 'It's Mrs Fortune's day. She can only come Tuesdays.'

'Oh, let's not work yet' said the Minister for Pollution.

'No, let's have a break eh?'

'Can we watch telly?' asked the Minister of Technology.

Click. '... the Royal Route lined and crowded – thousands here to pay tribute to the Royal Couple. And so as the gilt enamel of the Royal Coach leaves St James' Barracks, let's go over to Talbot Samuel at Westminster.'

'Well the tension here David is terrific. The crowd have been singing all morning; people have been coming and going; some have been leaving – not many; a few have been here all night; and each new arrival in the Lords has been greeted with a terrific cheer. There's almost a full house in there with over an hour to go. And so from a very festive Westminster, back to you David.'

'Well in fact we're going over now to take the 2.30 from Fontwell Park, its very waterlogged up there, three don't go, but the news is that the main race of the afternoon, the 3.15 Silver Plate, is definitely on, so if you've just switched on make a note of that. And we shall be covering that race as well. Well now with the latest news of the betting let's go over and join Norman Pidgeon on the course. . .'

The full banality of the BBC Sports Department was let loose on the Royal Event, for six hours. And ITV were no less predictable. Plumping for 'Divorce with the Stars' they had engaged Jonathan's Famous Television Personality to insult a variety of guests – film stars, famous cooks, lady novelists, television comedians, minor royalty, showbiz trichologists and desperate politicians – with his prepared adlibs, between flashes from the streets, live and as it was actually happening.

That was the television battle: royalty and showbusiness versus royalty and sport.

And for change on the other channel – on BBC 2 – rain from Lords.

'Turn the fleet?'
'Definitely.'
'Can we?'
'Yes technically.'

'Then we should.'

'We must. We're absolutely wide open.'

'Right. What if he doesn't stop at Cambridge?'

'Surely we can trust the Americans.'

Silence.

'I take it we're all agreed then that we shouldn't.'

Further silence.

'Very well then', said the Chancellor, 'I shall instruct the Admiralty to return the fleet as fast as possible. The country must be safeguarded. We must stand firm.'

Jeffrey entered the room.

'The President for you.'

'What President?'

'The President of the United States. On the phone.'

The Chancellor went pale. Then sat down. 'Er... I ... er.' He started to shake.

There was a pause. Jeffrey looked round the room. One by one they avoided his eyes. A long silence.

'Oh alright', said Jeffrey, 'I'll tell him you're out.'

He shut the door. Nobody spoke.

'Mr President.'

'Who's that?'

'I'm afraid the Cabinet are out sir.'

'Listen boy. Are you cleared for security?'

'Yes sir.'

'Promise?'

'Yes sir.'

'Scout's honour?'

'Yes Mr President.'

'All right. Listen. I want you to do something for me.'

'Yes sir.'

A pause. A sound of paper rustling. Does he spend ll day in there, Jeffrey wondered.

'Now listen, we've been getting some very strange eports from France and I want you to check your ellows – see if they've heard the same. OK?'

'OK Mr President.'

'Good man. Right. Call me back. Any time.'

'Oh Mr President.'

'Yes?'

'What do these reports concern?'

'That's a secret m'boy.'

'Oh.'

'Can you keep a secret?'

'Yes sir.'

'Good. All right then, we have heard a rumour here hat General de Gaulle is still alive. Are you still there?'

'Er yes sir.'

'Well?'

'But he died.'

'Yes, he died. But our information suggests that he ose again. Its an old trick, but it might just work. Check on it.'

Jeffrey put down the phone. He didn't know what to lo.

The forty two minutes were up. Staring anxiously down t their consoles in Mission Control the White Team, ne of the three maintaining twenty-four watch, re-orted that *Pelican* should be in view.

A minute went by.

Shirt sleeves, large glasses, third row down: 'Spain reports *Pelican*.'

'What's he doing?' asked Swineheart.

P I P : 'Hello *Pelican* this is Houston. Do you read me?.'

Pause.

P I P : '*Pelican* here. I am, go.'

Eye brows were raised. Jim Sickert was two minutes late reporting return of signal. Two minutes before making voice contact with Houston after forty-two minutes alone behind the moon. In those two minutes a sudden stream of imformation chattering into the computer banks told them he was alive. Each function of his body was taped, monitored with tiny transistorized electrodes that had started to signal the instant he came from behind the moon's radio shadow. Yet he had not spoken. Why the delay in reporting? Perhaps there was something in the computer information.

'Check body systems and life support systems.'

'Checking.'

While Jim Sickert was coming from behind the moon Mrs Jim Sickert was coming from behind, helped by the *Time* reporter. It wasn't much of a story to watch this astronaut's wife, hell, her man wasn't even going to the moon. Still it had its compensations. He bet Mrs Scheist and Mrs Grabowsky weren't so hospitable – too nervous; too many journalists too. They'd all be there, ten or more newsmen monitoring their reactions to the TV set. Why she'd been almost grateful for his intrusion. A real grateful lady.

At Houston they were puzzled.

'What's he doing?'

'I'm not sure.'

'Heartbeat's up. Look at his reactions. Pulse rate's high.'

Goggle eyes in shirt sleeves in the third row: 'He seems to be moving his wrist. That's the reaction I'm getting.'

'Jesus Christ!'

'What is it?'

'I think he's playing with himself.'

'What?'

'He's masturbating.'

'Eh?'

'Goofing off.'

'Well I'll be. . .'

'You're kidding.'

'Unless that machine's lying, its another first for America, fellas.'

'Wowee!'

The first space wank.

CODED TELEX. TOP SECRET. EX
ADMIRALTY HOUSE. TUESDAY 1530
HOURS. XYE 239687 VP
TO HOMEFLEET STEAMING
ISTANBULWARDS. STOP. COME HOME
SON LOVE MOTHER.

Very hot on signals, the Admiralty.

At precisely 15.42 the fleet came about for the third

time under the puzzled gaze of a Russian skipper. He stood on the bridge of a Russian fishing trawler which was heavily disguised as a battleship. No fools the Russians. Secretly, and contrary to all international naval regulations, this Russian ship had on board over two thousand barrels of fresh herring. Something like that could start a war. Now her skipper watched the entire British fleet in line astern start the huge circle that would turn them back towards Gibraltar; watched as they covered the same small sweep of sea for the fourth time.

'I thought so' said the Russian captain.

'Something the matter?' asked Sergei Tchaikowsky (no relation).

'All along I secretly thought so' said Skipper Prokofiev (no relation) in a wily Russian way.

'Thought what, Comrade Captain?'

'The English fleet.'

'What of them?'

'They're fishing.'

Lady Candida was at home recovering from the Flu. The whole group had taken her nearly two hours. Now she sat amongst the chintz at Number Eleven sipping tea and popping biscuits between tired lips. The strength of the girl! She set about her thousands with the jawbone of an ass.

'And where were you last weekend darling? Daddy and I missed you.'

'Oh I went down to the Country'. (A folk/rock sound – three fellows and a girl. She'd gone down to the girl too. It was a progressive group.)

'Daddy's quite worried about you.'

'Uhm, there's no need Mummy. Hey I had a part in a film.'

'Lovely dear, when's the premiere?'

'Don't know.'

Even if she did she couldn't take Mummy to see it. Nor could she tell her which part she had. Actually it had been the director's; and occasionally his stand-in's for close-ups. Two days in bed in an intellectual skin-flic for the Hampstead porno market.

'And what was it about dear?'

'Well actually it was based on a poem by Coleridge.'

'In Xanadu did Khubla Khan
A stately pleasure dome decree.'

If only S. T. knew what frenetic celluloid couplings his 'pleasure dome' had unleashed. Five days of fleshy filming. Most of it on the cutting room floor (the filming that is). She played Alph the Sacred River who ran through caverns measureless to man down to the silent sea.

'Hey, I'm really into that film scene.'

'Candida darling, you mustn't talk like that. It sounds American.'

The Chancellor popped his head in. 'Have you seen the model of the new airport?'

'Richard's got it upstairs darling. I said he could have it for his model railway layout. Was it important?'

'Yes a bit. They were going to build the third airport from it.'

'Oh. Well it might still be in one piece.'

'The Minister for Pollution's going spare. It's his baby.'

The Minister had indeed gone spare. Technology was trying to calm him down.

'We'll still build the airport, never you fear' said Pensions.

'Will we Home Secretary?'

'Definitely' said the Home Secretary, a gleam in his eyes that should have shown the watchers at the table that here was something more than a Home Secretary. 'No', he thought, 'they can't see it. My secret identity is safe.' Thinks: 'if only they knew.'

'Do *you* think we will Technology?' whined Polution

'Of course we'll build it.'

'Promise?'

'Promise.'

The Minister for Pollution was labouring under the misapprehension that his department was devoted to the promotion of pollution, in the same way that the Ministry of Agriculture is for the promotion of agriculture. Hence his policy of building airports in the green belt. Your airport is your number one polluter. It's tip top. Shit hot. Heaps better than an open sewer. In fact your ordure is a very second-rate type of polluter – many life forms even exist by it – yes very disappointing as an environmental poison. Reluctantly, the Minister for Pollution had concluded, on an official visit to a Brentford Sewage Farm, (which actually called itself 'The House at Pooh Corner'), that your average turd is a nourisher. He would stick to airports.

The bunting blew about the empty streets. The crowds were gone. Rubbish lined the Royal Route. Discarded souvenir programmes lay broken-spined in the gutters. Another Royal Day was done.

'I never thought *that* of him.'

'You can never tell. Not with a husband.'

'Poor thing. What will she do now?'

'Just be royal probably. Carry on being royal.'

'I wouldn't like their job. Not royalty.'

'No it's hard.'

'Still I had a good laff.'

'You've got to.'

'I like a jolly good weep at a wedding and a jolly good laugh at a divorce.'

'Looked radiant today.'

'Ooh lovely.'

'Beautiful I'd have said.'

'She looked nice too.'

'Always turned out well.'

'Still fancy him doing that with them.'

'You never can tell.'

'Not with Royals.'

'No. Anyway it were a good do.'

'Uhm yes. Better than a funeral.'

That evening Gibraltarians in their thousands turned out to watch the fleet passing for the fourth time. Sunday afternoon it had steamed proudly into the Mediterranean, full colours flying, saluting the Rock; only to return on Monday with barely a nod, scarcely a flag aloft, sleeves rolled up for action – suddenly recalled. Tuesday morning it had blushed past the Gibraltar cheers with scarcely a look in their direction, not a man visible on her decks as she steered uncertainly towards the warmer water. Unbelievably, that evening she'd returned, slinking past the jeers, painfully within distance of derisive hoots – the whole fleet steaming reluctantly once more out into the cold Atlantic.

It was enough to make Gibraltar Spanish.

Wednesday

At dawn the Yanks cut off Cambridge. Stealing softly into the silent streets, the road blocks were up before the sun. Bulky GIs embarrassingly over-dressed in quiet quadrangles chewed methodically, patiently, unquestioning, heavy automatics at their hips. The city rose to find itself besieged and occupied – efficiently, calmly, orderly but firmly overrun.

The convoys had roared in from Mildenhall and ancient Suffolk towns. Down rural roads they'd rumbled into Cambridge – tanks and armoured vehicles in the van. And then, sharp at ten, with the town secured and tanks dug in around it, they'd started the massive search for Communists. They knew what they were looking for. Methodically and with admirable patience they toured the dreamy spires and searched the gleaming towers. In college after college they paraded and checked mile after mile of corridor, alleyway, street, room, digs and house; searched and double searched for Communists.

But nowhere could they find any heavily-armed little yellow men in black pyjama suits.

Neither could General Atkinson. All day Tuesday Thailand had echoed to the screaming of jet planes, the whirring of the choppers and the thump-thump of artillery. Wowee! they'd moved so fast against Glade 6, tactically it had to be a knockout. But when they reached the scene of the crime – a dismal sort of place to die – not a single bloated body stirred, not a corpse, not a skull, not a rotten bleeding stiff. Nothing alive or dead. Only burnt grass and napalmed trees and not a single hired hand.

'Well they're making it authentic anyway' said General Atkinson as he spread the army wide to search and kill. 'Rotten little bastards.'

All day they'd fanned and spread and counter moved, the air alive with crackling orders, as the jets screamed low above them and their nerves got jangly in the prickly heat.

'Goddammit they gotta be here someplace.' complained General Atkinson peering at his mapboard, while icy fingers tickled up his spine. 'We've got to get them before dark. We've just got to.'

So they searched till night fell suddenly and left them camped apart in hasty bivouacs. Ten thousand sleeping men spread wide across the forests of Thailand; equipped with rocket, mortar, bomb and airplane, defending democracy against the Red and Yellow Peril who'd vanished like water into limestone.

And in the morning, still no trace. General Atkinson began to panic. As morning grew to midday and noon became lunch-time, General Atkinson started to squeak.

'Squeak squeak' went General Atkinson, his spine all frozen and numb.

'Perhaps they can't find us sir' suggested Sergeant OCC Megwinder.

The General stopped his squeaking.

'Ten thousand men, two hundred helicopters, fifty

jets all going every which way and you think they can't find us?'

'It was just a thought' said recently demoted OCC Megwinder.

At three, General Atkinson spoke to the President. 'It's a triumph sir' he said uncertainly.

'A triumph eh?' boomed the voice from the bathroom.

'In its way a great victory for American arms sir.'

'Really General Atkinson? Tell me how, so I can tell the press.'

'Well sir, it's like this. Without a single American loss, not one casualty, not one sir, we have entirely scared the enemy away.' Swallow.

A long pause.

'Arseholes!' said the President.

'Yes sir' said General Atkinson. 'However. . .'

But an angry yanking of an overworked flushing cistern terminated the discussion. General Atkinson started to compose his resignation.

'Jeffrey is the Commonwealth very important?'

'Very, Prime Minister.'.

'Well what would happen if they left it?'

'We wouldn't eat.'

'Oh dear. Jeffrey I don't like all this statesmanship. I haven't even got a Foreign Secretary to help me. Do you know Bobo and I haven't been sightseeing yet at all. I've hardly seen the poor lamblet since I got here, and then the Queen keeps phoning every minute. Jeffrey, what am I to do?'

'Speak to her.'

'Would you speak to her Jeffrey?'

'Why?'

'Well find out what she wants, then you can tell me.'

'She won't bite your head off.'

'Oh I don't know, she's bound to be beastly upset about the Commonwealth. After all she is Queen of all those countries in Africa, and if they go and leave because of me she's hardly going to call me darling. Be a love and tell her I'm busy. I am you know.'

'Yes, Prime Minister, I know.'

'Thank you Jeffrey, you're a dear.' The PM put the phone down unhappily.

'Good morning' said the Truce behind him.

'Ahhh!' screamed the Prime Minister jumping out of his seat.

'I hope I do not disturb the little white chief?' The truce of Noman beamed at his Commonwealth buddy cowering behind the curtaining.

'W-what do you want?'

'I merely came to pay my respects' said the Truce, touching his forehead and bowing backwards out of the room.

'Splendiman!' shouted the PM.

'Good morning sir, I trust the aggravations of the preceding day did not preclude the possibility of somnolent repose.'

'Thank you Splendiman, I slept well enough.'

'I am most felicitous in the hearing of it sir.'

'Why can't you keep that Truce figure out of here?'

'I'm sorry sir, I was down the corridor.'

'Why?'

'Tasting your breakfast sir. We mustn't have you poisoned by the foreign gentlemen sir, blimey, I'd lose my job.'

'That's very considerate of you Splendiman' said the Prime Minister, wasting his irony.

'You're very welcome I'm sure sir. I think you'll find there's nothing injudicious to the health included in the bill of fare.'

There was a knock at the door. Seaman Beal ingratiated himself into the room. 'Good morning Prime Minister.' He smiled.

Splendiman withdrew, leaving the PM picking at his breakfast tray.

'Well?' said the PM.

'You'll never guess what I've found out' said Seaman Beal.

And he probably never would have guessed except that Seaman Beal gave him no chance to see if he would or not for he launched himself with relish into his tale.

Not being one to waste a heaven sent opportunity Seaman Beal had decided to capitalize on the Commonwealth Conference. Not merely legitimately from the Hire of the hall, or illegitimately from the hire of the flesh that surrounded it, but in many other interesting ways as well. Now the most profitable of these sidelines was the ancient art and practice of incriminating photographs. In many circles, Particularly the diplomatic, this branch of the photographic world has developed into an industry. Basically it's simply a case of snapping the tempted whilst they enjoy the fruits of their temptation, facing them with the printed testament of their indulgence once repentance has set in and accepting largesse to prevent recriminations and the wrath-to-come from injudicious revelations of knowledge of same. In many ways it's the least unkind form of blackmail, for the victim has at least enjoyed something for his money. It could also be said to encourage honesty, for many a promising diplomatic career might have been saved by a frank encounter with the spouse.

'By the way darling I fornicated forty different sorts of ways with Oriental Annie in Kuala Lumpur whilst they filmed me from all angles for posterity.'

'That's all right Charles, the Farquarsons are coming round to dinner.'

But no, these things are still supposed to wreck a chap's career, and so he must be bought and sold into all kinds of naughtiness for the sake of a fifty-shilling fuck.

Now Seaman Beal knew this, and what is more he thought he had spotted the man most vulnerable. And so he equipped himself with hidden camera and photographic film and popped a popsy into Admiral Barrington's bedroom. She'd found the Foreign Secretary on the bed and stripped him in the darkened room without a murmur from his lips. No sound, no sign of protestation came from the Foreign Secretary. Then, bollock-naked herself, she started her performance before the connoisseuring camera-eye of Seaman Beal.

At first she'd merely posed in several indiscreet positions over and above the Admiral's body, whilst infrared magic-eyed its grainy images on the celluloid. But then, alarmed at the Admiral's frigidity, she'd attempted orally to raise a little life into his tepid pee-pee. Naught availed. Half an hour of lurid posturings, plaintive lickings, kindly kickings, hearty whippings, cursings, pantings, sucks and blows merely reduced the poor girl to puzzled exhaustion. Till finally, deeply offended by this unaccustomed customer-resistance she swore she would go no further, come who may. The Admiral, she declared, was no fun any more.

'And then we found . . !' said Seaman Beal, 'that he was dead.'

'It's most unfortunate' grieved the Prime Minister somewhat shocked by Seaman Beal's long tale.

'Not only dead, but stuffed. He's been a stiff for weeks. I've had to send the poor girl home. Very upset she was. That's necrophilia you know.'

'I know.'

'Carnal knowledge of a cadaver.'

'Poor thing' said the Prime Minister kindly. 'Please send her my condolences and half a dozen roses. Now what on earth are we to do?'

'Precisely' said Seaman Beal. 'You see I was going to blackmail him. Now that he's dead of course it changes things. I've got to blackmail you.'

'Oh dear' said the P M 'blackmail is such a dirty word.'

Not half so dirty as 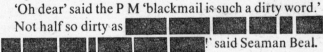 !' said Seaman Beal.

Back home Jonathan was blissfully busy with Numbers Six and Seven. He hadn't even meant it this way but Six and Seven had definitely worked together before. To give them their proper titles they were the middle daughter of the Minister of Technology and the youngest daughter of the Minister for Pollution, both, as Tory daughters sometimes are, ultra-left and neither yet past twenty. They'd approached him – a stroke of luck you need in Jonathan's line – and asked him to sign their petition outside Westminster. Quite a few groups were busy culling signatures in the crowd and theirs concerned a desperate attempt to stop the Government selling Turners to America for cash. (Desperate and unnecessary since half of them had gone and all the money was spent.) They'd asked him could they have his signature and Jonathan said yes, if he could have them, in a jokey sort of way, and they'd said yes and asked him where he lived. He'd told them and they'd said, 'See you later', turning up together at his flat and groping him whilst he signed. He hadn't meant together when he asked them both along, but they giggled and rolled him a spliff and rolled him gently into bed and told him he was nice and thanks for signing. The daughter of the Minister for Pollution said he couldn't have her in the front as she wasn't finally clear yet but he came in her ear and then in her mouth and she said if there was ever any doubt about the validity of his record he could have her properly any time. Jonathan, a past season ticket holder at a special clinic decided not to risk it.

They bathed together sometime later, all three uncomfortably cramped and then he'd watched their two damp bodies making gentle fireside love until he'd roughened with excitement and tumbled them both into bed. So there they'd fallen fast asleep to wake together in the morning, late and in a tangled heap.

Then they'd breakfasted and bathed again and dressed

and then undressed and – what the hell – got back into the unmade bed.

In the background, as they played, a repeat of 'Any Questions' steam-radioed its way through thickets of middle-class controversy to predictable conclusions – one good half-hour of it more damaging to the brain than a drunken lobotomist in a blackout. The Lady Deadwood, brown-voiced and velvet-smooth, ran the gamut of her prejudices; exercised her repertoire of thoughts as easily as her spaniels; paraded her inconsidered words considerately, each jaded thought much older than herself, handed down like heirlooms from antiquity. Out they came one by one in their stale majesty, applauded by a blood-curdling audience as they fell, the traditional English country virtues: bash the foreigners; flog the prisoners; ban the demos; fight the strikes; conscript the students; birch the borstal boys; keep the public schools; stop sex; start wars; halt nudity; castrate madmen; praise marriage; ban abortions; tax the pill; worship God; love animals; support the Tories; help Rhodesia; kill the stags; deport the blacks; and hunt the fox.

Jonathan, cunnilingering precious conservative pussy, simultaneously sucked superbly by the Minister for Pollution's daughter, herself reacting wildly to Technology's daughter's fingers, spared a thought for Lady Deadwood. If only she knew. What was she saying now?

'The immigration problem is like the problem of rats: too many of them and they start fighting . . .'

'Oh' said Arabella, above him, 'That's Mummy.'

'She's jolly good' said Felicity from his crutch.

'Don't speak with your mouth full' said Arabella.

'What a breed' thought Jonathan, tongue in cheek.

'Hey, don't stop.'

He took his tongue out of his cheek.

'Mmm thanks.'

'Mummy likes Daddy doing it in his riding breeches.'

'My Daddy can't do it.'

'How do you know?'

'He tried.'

'Really Arabella!'

'You should meet Mummy, she likes young men, ooh . . . especially when they do that.'

And so the three of them happily licking and fingering continued to listen to 'Any Questions'. As they were leaving Jonathan said, 'You must come again. . . .'

'Mm super.'

'Love to.'

'. . . next time we'll have "Any Answers".'

Vice-Admiral Haugh (pronounced variously like cough, rough, though, through and Slough) stared unbelievingly (and unpronounceably) at the small brown message in front of him.

CODED TELEX. EX ADMIRALTY HOUSE
STROKE DOWNING STREET STOP.
DOUBLE URGENT. MESSAGE READS.
GO ISTANBULWARDS ALL POSSIBLE
SPEED. MOST IMPORTANT
PRESTIGEWISE. REPEAT
ISTANBULMOSTURGENTGOWARDS.

The Vice-Admiral let out a great wounded bellow. On the bridge of the British flagship *'Return'* fourteen immaculately dressed officers and men studied the impeccable white of the floor.

'Arrgh!' shouted the Vice-Admiral. 'A-A-A-A-Arrgghh!' His fist started to pound the woodwork in front of him; his head banged rhythmically against the shatter proof glass. 'Ah-Ah-Ah-Ah-Arrgghhh!!!'

Fourteen fresh faces stared straight out to sea. The Vice-Admiral sank to his knees, tapping his temples against the polished metal in front of him. Nobody spoke. A very long time passed. Two tears started down the Vice-Admiral's cheeks, raced each other for his chin and plopped on to the floor.

Some more time passed.

At last the Vice-Admiral gestured gently with the buff message form. Reluctantly Commander Beste-Welcome spoke.

'Mr Richardson.'

'Sir.'

'Signal the fleet. We're turning round. We're going to bloody Istanbul.'

A choke. A strangled sob that was all. Nothing more. And then, 'Aye aye sir.'

From the signals rooms below came the sound of expensive equipment being smashed. Crash, crash, from the communications room.

'Excuse me gentlemen,' said Commander Beste-Welcome, 'I have to help the Admiral.'

But where in all the world are the RAF in this, you might well ask. Answer: an hour's flying time from Suez, in tight formation, heading straight for the Canal. At their head Wingco 'Fatty' Warwick happily humming the Dambusters March to himself. By Jove, this would be some wheeze. Show the chaps back home there's life in the old dog yet.

Wingco 'Fatty' Warwick was leading the RAF on perhaps the biggest raid since the Second World War. They were off to bomb the Suez Canal. The plan, and it was pretty well planned – he'd seen to that – had been conceived from an accidental find during their annual stocktaking. Someone in stores had come across a large number of wartime bouncing bombs, all carefully cocooned, as new, just sitting there waiting to blast a German dam into Cinemascope but unhappily frustrated by the untimely onslaught of civilities. What might a good old bouncing bomb do to clear a blocked up canal, argued the bored minds at the top, tired of forming squadrons of specialist flyers to race expensive planes towards each other for the titillation of the tourists. The Canal was important to the world, and there it lay blocked by rusting ships trapped along its length. An efficient airforce, or even the RAF, should be able to blast those ships out of the water, clearing the Canal and the political deadlock in one fell swoop. So they argued, and from there had grown the plan: a lightning raid down the length of it, blasting and bouncing bombs into every blocked-up ship –

several million tons of high explosive to shift a passage through de Lessops splendid Cut. Fifteen years work in a day.

And now the planes, big-bellied with their bouncing bombs, raced hard and low over the sea for the Canal.

'Whacko!' thought 'Fatty Warwick, 'Whata whopper wheeze.'

'They've landed on the moon' thought Sickert. 'Fuck 'em. I hope they can't get back.'

Four hours of circling ninety miles above the lifeless silence; four hours of listening to himself sing Annie Laurie whilst Houston molly-coddled the moon-struck motherfuckers; four hours and not so much as a hello Jim how-are-you-doing. 'Shit, I've a good mind to leave them there – boy would that teach those guys a lesson.' And he chuckled at the thought.

Houston had not called him since he'd achieved his particular space first, not through any feeling of neglect or even aversion – although whacking-off on your own in space was not high on the President's list of Space Priorities – no, it was simply that Houston in its infallible wisdom had been solely concerned with making sure that Scheist and Grabowsky landed safely, checked their relaunch systems and took their contingency geological sample. Sickert in the scheme of things was unnecessary now for two whole days. You don't pamper a machine.

The medical team, however, were interested in Sickert

and his wrist-experiment. Indeed they were itching to ask him all the how and why but no one dared while viewing millions watched in colour. What would the networks say? And they paid hard to carry this show to number two in the ratings. So the scientists had to sit back in this spectacular and ruminate on Sickert's palmistry.

Actually the truth of the matter was rather more mundane. Sickert did not do it for the hell of it. Behind his action lay the mighty sway of Madame Dollar, a little side-bet say, a kick-back, something to cheer him whilst the others grabbed the glory. Safe Rubber, a world-wide prophylactic company, had sponsored him to test their Filigree Condom in perfect weightless space conditions. Naturally he couldn't test it on a woman but in the birth control business improvization is the keynote; you have to keep one jump ahead. Several competitiors were already breathing down their neck of the womb and in business there is no place for sentiment or shame; besides, they knew it wouldn't make him blind. So Sickert had tested it and the result of his wrist-job would give them ten years start in rubber research plus a fortune for them all. Jim Sickert was not playing with himself, he was conducting a sponsored experiment for American industry.

'The Queen?'
'Yes, that's right.'
'No Madam, very sorry she not here.'
'I am the Queen.'

'Afraid must close now Madam. I tell her if she come.'

'Look here I *am* the Queen.'

'Oh dear Madam, I will tell most importantly as soon as sir comes in. Unhappily I not pronounce the tongue most well in no way.'

'Is that you Prime Minister?' asked a suspicious regal voice.

'No, no definitely not' said the Prime Minister in a very bad Indian accent, putting down the phone. That was close, she'd nearly rumbled him. Perhaps she had. Still, tough titty.

Seaman Beal stood to attention outside the door, beaming with pride. The Queen had used his telephone. The voice he'd heard down the line was Hers. She'd spoken to him, asked him for the Prime Minister. No slouch, he'd invited her to Istanbul – 'Come and see the Commonwealth Ministers whilst there's still a Commonwealth' – and what had she replied?

'Muh Prime Minister wouldn't let muh. Demmed fellow.'

He joined the PM in a little room from which he ran this bona bawdy house. Quite a little wizard with electrics Seaman Beal and what a box of tricks he had constructed. A big glass wall (mirror to you from outside) revealed the hall below where even now the Conference was in session . . . He flicked a switch; the sound drifted up . . .

'And I say to you Britain', a deep dark African voice said, 'that if you do this . . .' click. The Prime Minister switched him off. They were still addressing their remarks in full solemnity to the empty chairs and little wooden plaque marked 'Britain'; today not even the dead Foreign Secretary was there, and the PM was in no mood to hurry from the womblike warmth of Seaman Beal's control room. A miracle in itself this room: banks of TV screens, now dead, would give Beal instant replay in any room he liked; or he could plug the pictures through into a small dark viewing room where people who just watched could pay without contracting 'peeper's eye'. A comprehensive filing system, computer controlled, gave him details of his customers for their benefit, and occasionally for his. Accounts too were handled by this sophisticated ex-naval computer, for this was a credit-card establishment, a Barclaycard Brothel, AA recommended, four stars for comfort.

The fascia control panel ran at crutch height the length of the mirror/window, and amongst these switches, dials and knobs was the magic button, that on stag nights, or at special parties as a treat for very rich and welcome guests, converted all the mirror panels into glass, revealing to the hall all that went on behind the scenes. A hundred little rooms suddenly with their walls made glass all unbeknown to busy occupants. This effect, which justly made the brothel famous, was used only rarely, for the really rich – but what effect it had on parties, what a mine of customers it unearthed from what had been sedate dinner-jacketed occasions. Lasciviousness let loose, they streamed into the bookings room.

He'd once, and only once, displayed his grand effect to a mixed but very tight assembly. Everyone seemed happy at this wedding feast and Seaman Beal, uncharacteristically tipsy, with benevolence flooded the amazed guests with his hundred rooms of flesh. Right there it had started, right there in that Hall, the most spontaneous orgy by example he had ever seen. People fucking everything in sight. Ladies rampant with desire grabbing passing waiters to abuse them there and then. What a world of laying and sating went on before Seaman Beal's disgusted eyes. For it was all for free.

Oh yes he'd charged them extra for the breakages and the use of the waiters but he'd vowed he'd never again switch on his sights in mixed company. He who runs a brothel cannot afford to let folks fuck for free.

The tubby PM gazed down into the gilded hall in question and watched the delegates mouthing silent statements at the empty British desk. It's all bloody rubbish, he thought. Its all for the bloody press. And was that blondhead Bobo? Surely not.

'I'm sorry financial arrangements have to spoil our relationship, for you're a decent fellow' volunteered Seaman Beal, contemplating all that he possessed.

Yes, that was surely Bobo down below.

'For a PM, that is' – mustn't be too kind to a customer.

Who was that figure with him? Splendiman? No. Ah yes, the Truce. They must be looking for him.

'Yes, I trust the monetary aspect will not prevent us from being friends' inveigled Seaman Beal as the PM moved towards the door.

'Oh think no more about it,' said his paying guest, 'I won't have you shot or anything.'

The smile dropped straight from Seaman Beal's fat lips. He swallowed hard, then grinned, but the Prime Minister of Great Britain had left the room and Seaman Beal could not decide whether it had been a joke or not.

Blackmailers are particularly susceptible to being shot. It's not a pleasant thought – and as a breed it makes them nervous.

At Number Eleven Downing Street – 'So near and yet so far' the Chancellor had wailed on entering – a press conference was in progress. A group of hand-picked journalists were being plied with drink whilst their pockets were stuffed with hand-outs for their editors.

GREAT NEWS

The Ministry for Pollution proudly announces another great leap forward into the sparkling sunshine of technological advance. Yes this getaway jetaway decade sees another first for Britain's British businessmen – a spanking brand new airport, designed by top Scandinavian architects for the man who likes his business in New York, his dinner in Dusseldorf and his wife in Bermuda. Costing a mere forty million pounds this concrete and vinyl development project will be built in the heart of Berkshire near Sour End as soon as the hills have been levelled and the forest cut down. It will be the first air terminal in the world specially designed for the White Elephant, with the large double runaway needed to accommodate this superb twin-barrelled all-British Anglo-French achievement.

At Bristol forty white-coated technicians, as seen on television, registered a record noise level as the *White Elephant* passed by.

'Wow,' said one, 'that's fifteen decibels higher than the law allows.'

'And that's nothing yet' said another proudly. 'Wait till she takes off.'

In London Lady Candida was at last licking the lead singer of Cum (a super-group formed when Splat and Red Nasties split up so that they could express themselves individually). Happily, she worked away at the root of this talented guitarist in the offices of Great Barrier Reefers, an Australian musical consortium, whilst he, fellated, flicked through the pages of the music papers for his photograph. On the mantelpiece, as she squinted up to see how it was going, she recognized a life-size plaster model of his tool gold-plated – The Golden Groupie Award of 1974 – awarded by the Music Publishers and Friends of Israel Association for achieving a thousand groupies in one year.

In Cambridge the American armed forces had captured the entire staff of the San San Fook Chinese Restaurant. A line of puzzled waiters were being questioned about hostile troop movements in the town – in particular about a message found on one of them. It read:

A number 32
½ a number 37
a 14 special
chopsticks

   2 fried three delicious.

'Bombs away' said Winco 'Fatty' Warwick in a voice he'd heard a hundred times before – Richard Todd's. 'Da *dee* da da dah-dah da da da' he sang over the intercom. The Dambusters March. A beautiful melody by Eric Coates. 'Da dee da da da-da dum dum.'

'Bombs away' said Bombardier Rath, watching as they flew in low across the sweep of blocked-up sewage that used to be a waterway. 'The lower you are the better the bounce' Wingco Warwick had told them forty times within the week of crash-course training and they bellied in so low even the camels ducked.

Two hours before them, on a humane mission of mercy, a lone volunteer had piloted an ancient lumbering Shackleton along the path they would come, scattering leaflets to the few caretaker seamen left aboard the rotting hulks. 'Get out' it said in seven languages and four different sets of hieroglyphics. 'Get out before you're bombed' it warned – and get out they had got. You don't need two warnings when you've been trapped between Egyptians and Israelis for eight years.

Now the planes came in low in lines, and even now the first bouncing bomb had hit the water and, yippee, it bounced! There it went, three hundred miles per hour, skipping and jumping. *Bounce!* . . . it went again, all but leaping back into the plane from whence it had come, then down again and *Bounce!* . . . it started up once more. In great long strides it thumped its way down the Canal; behind it bounced its brothers. *Bounce!* . . . it cleared the superstructure of a ship by nearly sixty feet then down again and, *Bounce!* . . . it leapt again into the air and jumped a couple of stuck tugs without so much as looking down then, *Bounce!* . . . it landed short of S S *Anthrax*, cleared the gap above her bridge and leapt into the air again.

Bounce! . . . *Bounce!* . . . The narrow tract of sea was full of black and bouncing bombs. *Bounce!* . . . *Bounce!* . . . Until at last the leading bouncer landed smack upon the deck of S S *Curry* five years outward from Bombay. Expectant in their planes the RAF looked down to watch the massive vessel split and blow. But no, *Bounce!* . . . went the bomb. Quite undeterred it had struck metal, bouncing as sweetly as a ball on willow, smack! Racing for the next it hit the superstructure of a ferry half a mile ahead and glancing sharply from the blow it veered off sharply left, away into the desert. And there they watched amazed, as far away it bounced over dunes and sandy valleys, happily bounding until lost from view.

And now with sinking feelings in their hearts they watched the happy bouncings of their bombs, liberated from their years of cocooned disregard, set jumping through the Suez narrows, leaping through the salty lakes, occasionally changing their direction from stray touches on a vessel here and there, then heading gaily through the desert, bouncing fifty feet across a caravan of camels, their drivers' faces petrified with fear.

For two hours the RAF pursued their bouncing bombs, waiting vainly for the *crrump!* . . . that might at least have blown a ship apart. Two hours they watched and followed hopefully, without success – two hours longer than they should. For whilst they viewed with fatal fascination the cavortings and capers of their high explosive droppings they reached the point of no return and passed it by an hour. They could not now reach Cyprus on their fuel.

Grim-faced in the foremost plane Squadron Leader Gimlet stuck a needle into the quivering jelly that had been Wingco Warwick. 'We'll head straight south' he told his men pointing the small hand of his watch towards the sun and trying to bisect the angle.

The PM had found no trace of Bobo when he'd left the Seaman's room and feeling moral duty call he'd felt obliged to take his place in the Hall where mounting insults were heaped upon his head. He didn't listen much, but outside night began to fall and it seemed to him as if the talk was growing acrimonious. 'My word they really are upset' he thought. After an hour or two of dreamy thoughts of Bobo in a sauna he started to nod off and woke up later to find Seaman Beal sitting quietly by his side.

'I don't know how you stand the things they're saying about you' said Seaman Beal stoutheartedly. He wasn't racialist – he'd let any colour skin have any colour skin they wanted – but still their speeches were quite strong and he felt a little sympathetic towards the PM in his isolation.

'One gets used to it' said the PM deciding to pretend he'd been awake.

'I just popped in', said Seaman Beal, 'because I've

heard a rumour from communications concerning your RAF.'

'From the Foreign Office?'

'No sir, from *Triumphant*. We monitor the Russian Embassy.'

'For MI 5?'

'No sir, for Israeli Intelligence. They pay more.'

'Oh.'

'The thing is it looks as though the RAF have attacked the Suez Canal.'

'Oh no.'

'Apparently there's all hell let loose at the UN.'

'What's happening?'

'Well the Israelis and the Arabs have both claimed that Britain has intervened on their side.'

'Why?'

'The RAF attacked the middle. That's why nobody fired – they couldn't quite decide whose side they're on.'

'Ah.'

'Whose side *are* they on?'

'I've no idea' said the PM honestly. 'And, hell, I should know, I *am* the PM.' He was quite peeved.

'Another thing sir.'

'Oh really?'

'The Russians have denounced you sir.'

'I'm not surprised, I shall denounce the RAF myself.'

'No, not the RAF sir. The navy.'

'What about them?'

'They've been accused of fishing.'

'That's ridiculous.'

'My thoughts exactly sir. Oh, and one more thing.'

'Oh Seaman Beal, what is it now?'

'Something rather more light-hearted sir. Have you seen these?' And here he flashed a photo of a naked Bobo before the PM's eyes.

'He's tumbled me,' thought the PM searching in vain for his own likeness in the black and white. But no, he wasn't there.

'What a couple of jokers sir. Your Secret Service men are as queer as a couple of coots. Did you know you had a couple of benders looking after you?'

Naked as a baby Bobo stood – a perfect lissom youth. But who then was that in the background?

'Splendiman?' said the PM loudly.

'That's the chap sir. I reckon they're just about to play cross-hand boogie, don't you think so sir?'

The PM gazed hard at the photograph with all the tenderness and jealousy of a lover. Splendiman, not naked, but still, in his pyjamas and gazing hard with what looked like lust at what was definitely Bobo's bum.

'My word, they've certainly sent you a right couple to protect you – proper little married pair.'

Bells were banging in the PM's head, but no, the picture was not evidence. He could not say for sure that Splendiman was guilty.

'Do you mind if I keep this' asked the PM, pocketing it. It was a splendid view of Bobo and Splendiman could easily be cut.

'Why?' said Seaman Beal surprised.

'Oh, security, that sort of thing' said the PM confidentially.

'Ah' said Seaman Beal, nodding sagely.

'And I must say to you, Britain,' continued somebody,

'that unless you change your mind upon this issue, we shall expel you from our Commonwealth.'

Theirs indeed.

Night fell quite suddenly in the desert, giving no warning of its intense cold. Huddled together in the darkness lay a hundred planes – the British RAF in T. E. Lawrenceland, freezing on an isolated airstrip they had spotted just an hour before, when desperation rose to meet the thought of empty tanks, and big brave Biggles-dreams of ditching seemed a nasty necessity. Until amazingly there had suddenly appeared, like an oasis from the desert, a mile of concrete flattened strip. And here they'd touched down with relief, a hundred settling planes from out the sun. Where they were they had no idea, but here they'd stay, for though they had an airfield they'd no fuel. Still, at least they had a base, an RAF intact, not just a flotilla of little yellow rafts and a lot of bubbles where the planes had been.

The airfield was an oilfield strip, one of the many unlikely flats of concrete scattered through the desert where the drillers' bits had bitten oil. They could not see them now, but they should spot them in the morning, for a few small derricks lay behind the dunes not far away and here an Arab with a radio was trying to persuade his base that he was far from drunk and that a hundred British planes had just landed on his doorstep.

They were in Noman, Trucial State, land of the Lion's Truce, a smallish country of such wealth that they could buy the British Isles if ever they could flog the desert sand that made up Noman. But they could only sell concessions – your desert you can keep. So too thought three hundred marooned RAF men, shivering in its icy night and not yet having tasted the monstrous oven of its days.

Furore in the hall. Uproar – nothing less. That's what had greeted the PM's untimely peace formula to save the day for the Commonwealth. Bravely he'd slowly risen to their jeers and firmly he'd spoken, to silence them with a few words.

'What about a game of cricket, chaps?'

Nothing for at least a minute. Startled silence, and then such a clamour of derisive hoots, such a stamping, cursing, jeering, whistling mob of waving and complaining, such an angry shouting of abuse upon his head and all he stood for, that he had felt obliged to leave and sip a pint of lemonade whilst they had hastily composed a final motion for their show-down.

The press, by now excluded from the shindig, moodily received the drafted text, alerted London, stopped the presses, cleared the front pages. This was the final moment. They must wait outside.

'. . . such an assurance not being forthcoming from Great Britain, no such undertaking having been received, then the Commonwealth has no alternative but to invite Great Britain to withdraw from membership of the Association.'

That was it, exclusion stuff. The order of the boot. The bullet. The grand pissovsky of them all. By now they'd started voting; ten for the motion already, If that figure reached eighteen the Commonwealth was no more. Eighteen, the magic number, the two thirds majority required.

'Fourteen, the teller intoned as the PM took his seat.

'Australia' called the chairman slowly.

'Australia says "No".'

(Good white support there, the PM mused.)

'Canada' the chairman called.

'Canada votes "Yes".'

(Half stinking French.)

'Fifteen' called the teller.

'Zambia' the chairman said.

'Zambia says "Yes".'

(Predictable, thought the PM. Cut their bloody allowance.)

'Sixteen' called the teller.

'New Zealand.'

(Great white hope again.)

'New Zealand abstains . . .'

(Bleeding Maories. No good there, Sixteen still.)

'Tanzania.'

'Yes.'

(Of course. The game's up. Goodbye Commonwealth.)

'Seventeen', told the teller.

(Goodbye Queenie. Goodbye job. Oh piss.)

'Noman' called the chairman in a voice of doom.

There was a hush over the assembly. This was it. They'd read about these moments, a genuine piece of history, now they were part of it. Fascinated by themselves they sat rooted.

Will he, won't he, wondered the PM, looking at the

Truce. What a way to go.

'Noman' called the chairman testily.

The Truce stood. A vast wall of silence focussed around him. The delegates had ceased to breathe. This was it.

'Noman says. . .'

'Wait!'

A burst of murmurs, a turning and a craning of necks. Who had spoken so commandingly? It sounded a bit like . . . surely not?

'Wait' repeated the Prime Minister, his voice steady with authority. This is what it's like to be an actor, he thought, the still centre of attention. Time had become something very slow, he could feel it passing as in the moment of a car accident, between the braking and the crash when everything seems frozen within a quarter of a second. His mind was racing now.

An even vaster hush fell. The great baroque brothel hall waited in silence for its redeemer.

'Prime Ministers, ministers, delegates, gentlemen.' (I've no idea what I'm going to say, he thought, listening in amazement to himself. I've not a clue. I don't even know why I'm on my feet.) 'Before the voting on this issue continues I feel there is something you should know.'

(Look at them, wrapt in attention, hanging on my every word. I've got them all in the palm of my hand. A captive audience. They want to know. What? What ever I tell them.)

'Something that concerns us all deeply . . . *(pause)* . . . Vitally . . . *(pause)* . . . and must have a profound effect on all of us here today on this historic occasion.'

(Steady. A slight ripple. Be careful, they're going.)

'Gentlemen!'

(They're back.)

'Gentlemen I must inform you ...' (What? What shall I inform them? This is it. Oh what the fuck ...)

And then a flash. A genuine inspired flash, as if some part of his subconscious took pity on his plight and sent his instincts to his aid.

'My Foreign Secretary, Admiral Sammy Barrington, is dead.'

A deep gasp throughout the hall. They were with him. The PM held up his hands for silence.

'He died ... because of us ... *(pause)* ... because of you.'

Silence.

'We killed him. All of us. Here in this hall we murdered him as surely as if we had stabbed him to death. His blood is here in this room. His blood is on our heads. His blood is on our hands. His blood is on our conscience.'

A low wail from the back of the hall, a moaning sound.

'He died because he couldn't bear to see this great organization die.'

Sobs. Genuine sobs. Wet eyes were everywhere.

'He is dead because he could not live to see his Commonwealth dead. He could not bear his life without the life of all of us together in one brotherhood of nations. And so we killed him. We denied ourselves to ourselves.'

A keening softly in the echoes of the hall.

'This great man ... whose life blood *was* the Commonwealth had seen that life blood start to spill into the gutters.'

'No, no, no, no.' A rocking, wailing sound of grief.

'And so we killed him. His friends and colleagues over many years, *we* caused his death.'

There were tears in Seaman Beal's eyes. 'Beautiful,' he said, 'beautiful.'

'And shall we kill him twice within one day?' The rhetoric echoed round the hall. 'Shall we hack away at his memory until we've cut out every living thing we hold together?'

'No' came a deep throated moaning chorus.

'Shall we, killing him, now kill what most he loved?'

'No, no.'

'Shall we who murdered him now turn and kill our Commonwealth, rip down our rules, throw out our Sovereign Queen and poison all we hold most dear?'

'No, no, no,' said the assembly. Open tears now flowed across the crowded room.

'Gentlemen, I beg you. In your mercy, reconsider.' And he sat down.

A great silence. Then a growing thumping, a fast drumming quickly swelling, a tapping of tables rhythmically. The sound flew round the room encompassing delegate after delegate. A great pounding of fists, of feet, of anything – a mounting pyramid of noise that grew towards a peak. They were united in the noise. No speech, no sound of voice; a primitive rhythmical pounding of their grief, of their emotion held in common. They were together in the sound. Thumping hard they saluted the oration, they dumbly praised the dignity of the speaker, they had found someone to lead them. It was an affirmation. Louder and louder swelled the drumming – thump, thump, thump, thump – hands on tables, feet on floor. Thump, thump, thump, thump, growing stronger by the minute and still no end in sight. Thump, thump, thump, thump, joined in Seaman Beal, tears flowing down his cheeks. Checkmated the Conference and him. He was a craftsman, Seaman Beal, and knew the beauty he had seen. Thump, thump, thump, thump, his hands pounded on the wooden fascia of his control box.

The rhythm now was deafening. The mirrored hall gave back the sound and magnified it. A prison on the evening of an execution, a thousand minds protesting with one sound: the clank, clank, clanking of the pipes – even so this thumping clamoured for some expiation, appealed in vain for some release. Let this great weight be lifted.

Thump, thump, thump, thump, went Seaman Beal.

Thump, thump, thump, thump, the delegations.

And then he did it. Smack! Palm against the mirror release button. His effect. In an electric instant the power of a thousand volts sped through the cunning circuits, shifting mirror into glass, reflections into air, revealing through the lately mirrored walls, now panelled glass, a moving tapestry of flesh. A hundred gilded rooms activated into life; a hundred rooms caught unawares, their occupants still thrusting, all unknowing that they stood and lay and sat and crouched and knelt revealed through one-way glass. And in each room what frenzied scenes of orgiastic lust; what obscene pageants everywhere, by twos and threes and by the roomful; what piling bodies meshed in flesh; what heavings of great buttocks; what bosoms sucked and bounced and bundled; what secret growths of hair amazingly revealed wet-lipped;

what private parts so publicly displayed, in fifty different sorts of posturings. A living lithograph of lust around the shell-shocked congregation.

What a *coup de theatre!* From all sides wild applause broke out – pandemonium. They ran about the room applauding, gazing, pointing, cheering, smiling, laughing, nudging, watching: a great catharsis in the Commonwealth. And there the PM sat, the great originator of it all – amazingly quite unaware – the very picture of a man transformed into a hero. They carried him about the room, a vast procession forming behind and then they burst between the double doors – the cheering delegates on their heels – and out into the vestibule. The entire press corps was dumbfounded, presented with a dreamlike vision: the British PM borne aloft on stout black shoulders at the centre of a cheering tumult, crying, weeping, singing and wailing that followed him and called his name and hallooed his praises.

Into the town the bewildered press followed the procession, snapping, photographing, noting, writing, but uncomprehending what was happening. In front of the Gallipoli Hotel the stamping multitude of diplomats stood and sang and danced together, whilst the PM from his balcony looked down on them and waved.

> 'Land of hope and glory,
> Mother o-of the free.'

Flash, flash. Click, click.

> 'How shall we ex-tol thee,
> Who are borne of thee!
> Wider still and wi-der . . .'

'*Is* Splendimen having Bobo?' wondered the Prime Minister.

Thursday

Jonathan woke up with Number Eight exhausted. He was, she was and they were. I'm going to give up married ladies he thought, they don't have enough of it. They seem to have spent half their lives celibating.

To be perfectly honest, Number Eight, the Foreign Secretary's daughter was a bit of a dog. Lucy Scott-Fox-Harrison (née Barrington) possessed that sort of English rose beauty that gets blighted early but which at fourteen tempts the mind with promises of sin at the expense of magistrates and courts. Twenty years and seven hundred copies of *Harpers and Queen* and *Vogue* later they've lost their early bloom for that Paris-original Harrods-account, head-scarved thoroughly well-groomed look. The female equivalent of a well turned out race horse. So what becomes of all those upper middle class Lolitas? Having escaped by the skin of their hymen from an early public school entanglement they usually fall victim to a bounder in the bushes at a ball. Completing a season that dances between Queen Charlotte's Ball and Queen Charlotte's Maternity Hospital they steer away from sex into the homely harbour of a business marriage with a nice man, a steady man, a Nigel or a Neil, who likes his loving, gently, infrequently, in darkness. And here their puppy fat grows up into Alsatians while their minds are beaten flat by the connubial banter of a commuter-husband who only reads the *Telegraph* and only speaks *Financial Times*. Till one day when they exercise their conscious will for the first time in fourteen years by leaving poor old Nigel or poor Neil to drink himself painlessly to death in the Long room Bar at Lords, they embark upon a rash of badly judged affairs with ageing Irishmen and portly Chelsea writers who beat them when they're drunk and call it real feelings. And so to Analysis and Alcohol – twin pillars of their world and thus the product of your upper - middle - income - class anglo - saxon marriage – a clutch of randy thirty-six-year-old divorcees with their muddled teenage minds rubbing off against a feeling they've missed out somewhere and a determination to leap before they look.

Lucy Scott-Fox-Harrison, treble barrelled and unloved, fucked desperately away at Jonathan, whilst outside a rather sneering little weaseled-faced man took note of all the hours she'd spent inside so 'poor old Nigel' could get custody of her children.

'Enough's enough' said Jonathan at ten, to the late Foreign Secretrary's daughter as he left her spreading nakedness in his bed to wrestle with the coffee-grinder.

'Daddy's being dumped today.'

'What?'

'They're dumping Daddy in the water today.'

'It's not dumping,' said Jonathan, 'it's burial at sea.'

'It's still dumping. It's inside the harbour. It's not healthy. Why do they have to do it so quickly anyway?'

94

'Must be because of the heat.'

'Oh.'

'Still that is quick. He only went yesterday.'

'Good heavens no, he's been dead for months.'

'What?'

'He's been a stiff for months, they've been carting him about stuffed. Terrible isn't it?'

'Are you serious?'

'Of course I am.'

'But good heaveans. . .'

'Cunning bastards aren't they.'

'But that's disgraceful' said Jonathan outraged.

'Absolutely' agreed Lucy. 'Another two months and we'd have been able to avoid death duties.'

Morning fell in Istanbul. That's precisely the way the PM felt it – he'd a splitting tummy and his head hurt. They'd forced the celebrations down his throat in liquid form until he'd reeled away and left them dancing gaily through the streets. The airmail paper of the morning *Times* shouted out his praises to the skies through which it had arrived.

There was no knock at the door. 'Good morning little white chief' announced the Truce of Noman in a deafening voice. The little white chief could only indicate his sickness and his unwillingness to testify to the goodness of the morning by drawing the coverlet over his head.

'I hope his diplomatic triumph has not entirely exhausted the British Prime Minister' said the Truce, thoughtfully revealing all his ivory teeth.

'What do you want?' said the PM like a pouting ten year old.

'I've brought a document we signed last night' said the Truce, unrolling the white linen of a cafeteria tablecloth which was covered in scrawls of scratchy handwriting endorsed beneath by many shaky hands.

'I took the liberty of drawing up this memorandum during the festivities. It's been signed by everyone but you.'

'What does it say?'

'It's a peace formula' said the Truce. 'We thought of quite a good way to save your face and the Commonwealth.'

'Oh' said the PM, wondering how he could save his head.

'The agreement allows you to sell your tanks, although we register our disapproval naturally.'

'Naturally' said the PM, thinking of Seltzer.

'But there is one proviso.'

'And that is?'

'You secretly agree not to sell them any ammunition.'

'No ammunition.'

'Precisley.'

'But they won't be able to get any if we don't sell it them. They're British tanks, they *need* British ammunition.'

'Precisely. Furthermore, you guarantee to us you will not supply them any spares.'

'Isn't that rather diddling them?' asked the Prime Minister.

'Of course not. Its a fair business deal.'

'By Jove I think you're right' said the Prime Minister scenting compromise. 'This would work.'

'Of course it'll work. It only needs your signature.' The PM searched for his ball-point and added his fine italic.

'By the way,' said the Truce, rolling up the secret memorandum, 'the Foreign Secretary *is* dead?'

'Oh yes.'

'How are you . . . disposing of the remains?'

'Burial at sea. Today. The quicker the better.'

'Oh. I see.' The Truce sounded slightly disappointed.

'Why?'

'Well I just wondered if. . .'

'What?'

'It is an ancient custom in our land. A mark of respect you understand.'

'What is?'

'When somebody important dies. It is a custom . . . so that his strength and wisdom may be inherited by all those who. . .'

'Yes?'

'Who join the feast.'

'Who what?'

'Who attend the . . . banquet.'

'Who what?'

'Who join in at the the table after he's been . . . cooked.'

'Do you mean who EAT HIM?'

'Yes, Prime Minister.'

'Splendiman. SPLENDIMAN!!'

The Truce began to back away. 'It is a custom,

nothing more.'

'SPLENDIMAN!'

'A mark of respect. An act of piety.'

'GET HIM OUT'

'A religious duty. A festive observation.'

'Splendiman!'

The Truce had gone.

'Breakfast!' said Splendiman bringing in the tray. The PM puked into the basket by his bed.

'I'm sorry sir' said Splendiman.

'Take it away' said the Prime Minister.

'Its perfectly harmless sir, contains nothing poisonous. No dead bodies in it' he said to cheer the Prime Minister up, and failing dismally.

The PM threw up again.

'Is something the matter sir?' Splendiman asked brightly.'

'That man' said the PM palely.

'The Truce. Was he in here again?'

'He was, Splendiman.'

'What did he want?'

'He wanted to eat our Foreign Secretary.'

Splendiman looked at the food he still held in the tray and went bright green.

'Excuse me a minute sir.' Sounds of flushing from the bathroom.

The telephone rang.

'Yes?' said the pallid PM.

'I would like to speak to my Prime Minister. This is the Queen.'

The PM went a little paler.

'Hello. Hello. Oh hell I've been cut off. Hello are you

there Istanbul? Hello. Dammit. Operator!'

Slowly he replaced the receiver. When would she leave him alone!

Splendiman appeared at the bathroom door.

'Where's Bobo?' he was asked.

'I couldn't rightly ascertain the answer to that interrogative sir' said Splendiman, a faded shadow of his former self. 'They came and moved him from our room last night sir, moved him into somewhere else.'

'Good' said the Prime Minister viciously, thinking of that photograph. 'You keep your hands off, mush,' he thought, 'he's mine.' But he didn't say it. Not to Splendiman. Not now. The thought of the two of them was too incongruous. He couldn't have. He wouldn't have.

'I wonder where the RAF is' said the Prime Minister after a while.

The RAF was in Noman's Land. Stalag Luft V they'd called it. They'd been surrounded early by a force of forty Arabs who, though armed and hostile-looking, had treated them with kindness and had pitched them tents to guard against the sun.

The RAF reacted to captivity with all the pent up joy of twenty-five years peace. This at last, was it. Already they had formed an escape Committee and started to tunnel. Busy groups of burrowers moled their way in four hour shifts from every corner of the camp, while active sports and games, and healthy keep-fit classes were everywhere as decoys. The Arabs watched them in amazement. First thing, they'd built a wooden horse and while two men dug frenetically into the crumbling sand inside, twenty-five men lumbered sweatily over the great wooden beast, as the sun rose high in the sky.

Another group played basketball, keeping cavey for a hidden five and nearby, ten more airmen, their pockets full of sand and holes, wandered happily up and down scattering all the freshly excavated stuff from yet another tunnel. The temperature was well into the eighties and it was not yet ten o'clock as the Arabs watched the busy movements of the RAF maintaining their morale.

The senior sane British officer (Wingco 'Fatty' was still blubbering) had already officially surrendered to the Arab leader, explaining politely but firmly in German that they would give only their names, ranks and serial numbers. (Oh, and planes too since they already had them.) The Arab leader answered him politely in the German tongue, that he had read Political Economy at Oxford (before the Home Secretary had made him leave), that he would appreciate some tea, and would he like to speak in English as he was afraid his German was a little rusty.

Somewhat put out, Squadron-Leader Gimlet had consented, although he persisted in referring to Harish Hashish El-Nordern as 'the goon'. It was perhaps to make himself feel a little better about the Arab's University career. (Gimlet had been turned down by Oxford and had been obliged to cram his way into Cranwell with the other drop-outs.) Later he asked 'the goon' if they might hold a camp concert when the sun got lower, and wondered if the Arab force would be so good as to be their guests. Harish Hashish El-Nordern said that by the soles of his grandmother's boots he would be delighted to attend, adding that many desert winds had blown since he had seen a decent show. (It was in fact the Alexandrian version of *Fiddler on the Roof,* a slightly remodelled Arab adaptation, where the happy Jewish family voluntarily promise to leave Palestine at the end of the last act.)

Squadron leader Gimlet, unhappy with this friendly social interchange, steadfastly refused to hear El-Nordern's version of a Peter Cook monologue he'd heard originally as cabaret at a Commem. ball and smartly put the feller in his place by demanding separate quarters for the officers. The British class system must be preserved, not *even* but *particularly* in the desert.

'. . . Still no news of the missing British RAF which yesterday attacked the Suez Canal. Both Arabs and Israelis have welcomed the British action which they claim is timely intervention on their side.

'In the United Nations yesterday, a Russian resolution condemned the British fleet for fishing instead of, quote, behaving in a proper warlike manner as laid down under the terms of the Geneva Peace Convention.

'Scheist and Grabowsky are still major news on most of the world's papers and there's plenty of front page pictures of their moon-walk. Well, I guess that's about all the news from Houston as of this time, so I'm out.'

'Scheist and Grabowsky in the news. What about Jim Sickert?' thought Jim Sickert miserably. 'There they are gambolling about on the moon – hell, I've always wanted to go to the moon – and what have they done since they've been there? Nothing but turn the damn TV cameras on each other. They're worse than a couple of faggots with their cameras — dammit, they're just ego-maniacs. They don't deserve to get up off that moon at all. My God, if I had a mind to it nothing in the world would force me to pick them up tomorrow. Boy, would they be in trouble? All technology and basically what does it come down to? Me. If they don't dock and I don't rendezvous they can forget all about it. Ain't nothing they could do. It all depends on me. Hey that's quite a point' he thought. Something was beginning to stir in his mind. Ten minutes passed whilst Sickert sat considering.

P I P : 'This is Houston. Come in Jim.'

'Ah so they think I'm still alive. Very good of them to speak to me I'm sure.'

P I P : 'Houston to *Pelican*. Do you read Sickert?'

P I P : 'Affirmative.'

P I P : 'All systems set for rendezvous technique?'

P I P : 'No.'

P I P : 'What do you mean, negative? Please clarify.'

P I P : 'Just no.'

With a click the television channel to communications was turned off. Something was obviously wrong. Bye viewers.

P I P : 'Would like information on the negative.'

P I P : 'Houston can get stuffed.'

P I P : 'Are you feeling all right?'

P I P : 'I'm feeling fine thank you.'

P I P : 'What's the problem for the rendezvous Jim?'

P I P : 'The problem is there ain't going to be no rendezvous.'

The clear voice echoed round the mission control centre. Technicians looked at each other blankly. Was this human computer failure, technological breakdown in homo sapiens?

P I P : 'Why not Jim?'

P I P : 'Because I say so.'

P I P P I P : 'This is Andy Scheist, Jim, I guess we heard that. What's the problem?'

P I P : 'The problem, dear Andy, is that you make me puke.'

P I P : 'Houston, Jim. Will you take one of those A42 capsules in the medico locker. We think you might have caught a little flu.'

P I P : 'Roger yourself, Houston.'

P I P P I P : 'Er, Jim, this is Richard Grabowsky. I expect I don't have to remind you I am Mission Commander.'

P I P : 'No, dear Richard, you do not. What are you recommending for my flu, chicken broth?'

P I P P I P : 'What is the matter Jim?'

P I P : 'I ain't picking you up tomorrow.'

P I P P I P : 'In heaven's name why not?'

P I P : 'Not until I get two million bucks.'

HEAVY STATIC

P I P P I P : 'That's blackmail Jim.'

P I P : 'Affirmative. Out.'

'Congratulations Prime Minister.'

'What on?'

'For last night, sir, saving the Commonwealth.'

'Oh that. Thank you dear boy.'

'The papers here are full of your praises. You've got every front page. You've even beaten the astronauts.'

'Photographs Jeffrey?'

'Yes, in them all.'

'Nice ones of me?'

'The best.'

'Oh good. My mother will like that.'

'Your personal rating has gone up thirty per cent. Its now at thirty-five per cent.'

'That's higher than it's ever been.'

'Yes, Prime Minister, there's nothing you can't do now. Everybody's very excited over here. They're throwing a special gala evening for you on Saturday in the Albert Hall. Some of the papers are even calling you a Churchill.'

'I will not tolerate blasphemy, Jeffrey.'

'They mean it nicely, sir.'

'Jeffrey, the most horrible thing happened this morning. The Truce of Noman came to see me.'

'Oh, by the way, congratulations on that agreement. The Foreign Office are studying the text in detail but it seems a tremendous compromise, sir. How did you think of it?'

'Oh, er, it came to me. Listen, I was telling you about the Truce. Do you know he offered to eat our Foreign Secretary.'

'What, raw?'

'No, cooked.'

'You're not going to let him, I take it.'

'Jeffrey!'

'Sorry.'

'And the other beastly thing that's happened is what I warned you about. I hold you entirely responsible for this, Jeffrey. You made all the arrangements.'

'What's happened?'

'Bobo and Splendiman have happened.'

'Bobo and who?'

'Splendiman.'

'Good God he's not a . . .'

'Yes Jeffrey? Not a what?'

'Well I mean . . . *is* he?'

'I'm not sure. But I suspect he's been tampering with Bobo.'

'Oh I doubt it sir. With respect.'

'Bobo's very tempting you know. In many ways he's almost . . . well *I* know it's charm, but it looks a little like . . . well, flirtation.'

'Well you'd better have it out with Splendiman.'

'Yes, I will.'

'Tackle him about it. I mean we can't have . . . We must be careful of Bobo.'

'Thank you Jeffrey and bless you for saying that. You know there have been times when I thought that you did not altogether wholeheartedly *adore* Bobo.'

'Sir!'

'Times when I positively thought you never even cared for him. Thank you Jeffrey. I'm very touched.'

'Yes sir.'

'Goodbye Jeffrey.'

'Goodbye. Oh sir, the Queen's been trying all . . . ' But the line had gone dead. Jeffrey picked up the papers. Aside from the PM's triumphant headlines there was only trivia. From one of his two houses, a Cabinet

Minister had accused an £18 a week worker of holding the country to ransom. The Home Secretary had deported another foreign student – this time an Australian – for attempting to read Politics at the University of West Anglia (where even the Dean is Special Branch). Very decent fellow the Home Secretary. 'I couldn't in all conscience ask him not to read Politics as this would have been an intolerable constraint on his personal liberty. The only decent honest course open to me was to throw him out.'

'Why will there be no independent inquiry?' someone had the gall to ask him.

'I'm afraid' said the Home Secretary, 'I cannot comment on that until it's been officially hushed up.'

Jeffrey chuckled – Wily b... the Home Secretary. He was just beginning to congratulate himself on handling Fleet Street beautifully when his eye fell on a small paragraph: C A M B R I D G E   O U T R A G E

'Oh Hell' he thought. But it was not too bad. It hardly mentioned the occupation.

> The British Hoteliers Association have threatened the Americans that unless the Chinese waiters are released in Cambridge, reprisals will be taken against the American waitresses at the Mighty US Hamburger Joint in the Kings Road. The restaurant is owned and run by American millionaire playboy and racing yatcht, Norman Pules 111.

'I'll get the CIA on to Pules for this' thought Jeffrey. 'He's done it for publicity. By God I'll bust his parties.'

'Who is 2 Fried Three Delicious?' said the boy from Iowa Military Intelligence College to the waiter from Kow Loon and San San Fook Foodstufs Cambridge Ltd.

'Sir' said the waiter blankly.

Four hours now of intensive interrogation.

'Who is 2 Fried Three Delicious?'

'I bring' said the waiter. And he brung. The boy from Iowa did not appreciate the joke. He had a big gun and this ignorant Chink instead of bringing him the man he wanted had brought him a bowl of rice.

'Don't play games with me.'

'You want play game?' said the waiter, not fully conversant with the language, let alone American.

'Chess?' he asked the limited Intelligence Officer. 'D'laughts? Mahjong?'

The boy from Iowa pondered these answers and wrote them down. Now they were getting somewhere.

'Splendiman' said the Prime Minister, finally determined to put an end to all this doubt. Jeffrey was quite right.

'Sir.'

'Splendiman . . .'

'Yes sir.'

'Splendiman . . . er. Are you . . . er. Look here.'

'What is it sir?'

'Splendiman. Are you queer?'

'No sir, I'm not. But thank you very much anyway for asking.'

'Good God,' thought the PM, 'he thinks I'm propositioning him.

'Good God,' thought Splendiman, 'he's fallen in love with me.'

'I wish to speak to the British Prime Minister.'

'I'm afraid he's in Istanbul' said Jeffrey. 'Who shall I say called?'

'The President.'

'Oh hello sir. It's me.'

'Hi.'

'How are things?'

'Very bad m'boy. Hey you're not a soldier?'

'No sir, 'Fraid not.'

'Pity. I'm looking for a good General for South East Asia.'

'Er . . . ' said Jeffrey.

'What was that?'

'That's an excellent force of yours in Cambridge.'

'Good are they?'

'Excellent reports from our side, sir. Resourceful. Brave. Above all, sir, tactful.'

'Good, good.'

'You don't think they should go to . . . '

'Hey why don't I send those boys to Asia.'

'Very good idea sir.'

'Thank you m'boy. Yes of course its a good idea. We don't need them in Cambridge. Whoever heard of good American soldiers in Cambridge. Its ridiculous.'

'Exactly sir. Your back door's quite safe in our hands.'

'Back door?'

'For the Normandy landings sir.'

'Oh yes, that. Well there's a bit of trouble in that direction.'

'Political?'

'No, casting. Elizabeth Taylor won't do it, Barbara Streisand's tied up with the remake of *The Sound of*

Music, and Warners are threatening to withdraw their money . . . hey!'

'Sir?'

'Do you think your Queen would be interested?'

The funeral of Admiral Barrington was at three. The late Foreign Secretary was being laid to his final resting place in accordance with his own wishes – burial at sea. Well, not quite sea, but water anyway. 'Dumped in the harbour' as his sexually excessive daughter had called it. In fact it was the outer harbour which was deep and practically the sea anyway, and he would be dumped from the deck of the Royal Navy's finest aircraft carrier *'Triumphant.'*

At precisely 2.30 the Prime Minister and his party were welcomed aboard the mighty ship by Commander Gwen MacPherson – an unusual name for a Scot but quite appropriate. He'd flown directly from his home and friend in the south of France the moment the news had come through and he'd arrived in time to stage-manage the affair. Burial at sea had seemingly attracted the entire civilian population of Istanbul who lined the harbour walls and thronged five deep beside the quais. The harbour itself was filled with tiny boats packed with people who at 2.00 had had the quite additional thrill of seeing the Royal Helicopter, shockingly horrendous in wrong red, alight on the *Truimphant's* flight deck. Stepping sprucely from inside the *deus ex machina* class B helicopter the Royal Son and Heir was escorted to the ward room by Commander Gwen himself.

Triumphant herself was a triumph. Above the waterline she was everything a fighting ship should be, and who could see below? Her decks were lined with sailors splendid in their whites, specially given the day off by Seaman Beal so that they could be on board. (The golden bordello was running on a skeleton crew for the duration of the burial.) Flags of all nations fluttered happily from the ship and bunting was displayed about the quayside. The harbour, dressed and sundrenched, had a festive air. It looked more like a regatta than a funeral.

Aboard, in the centre of the flight deck, an enormous black hole showed that the vast square lift to the hangar deck was down, and deep inside this shadowed hollow, underneath a British flag, an enormous oaken coffin lay. Inside this, Admiral Barrington, secure in first-class British oak, with first-class Brummy brass handles and the lot handmade.

The embalmers had had no need to work their magic on the Admiral for the miracle of taxidermy still survived, so that they'd simply screwed him down into his air-tight box and marched him proudly to his last but one resting place on the lowered flight deck lift of HMS *Triumphant*.

The Commonwealth was naturally finely represented: some a little pallid from the previous night's excesses, yet most had made an effort and had dressed in national costumes giving the affair even more the look of a carnival. The PM, sharp at half past two, in a sober suit with suitable black tie was piped aboard the ship. He missed the muffled drum, the slow march through the rainy streets behind the rumbling gun carriage. There was altogether too much sun for such a solemn day, he thought, though even he was taken by the beauty of the harbour. Such a pity that the navy hadn't made it.

The Band of the Royal Marines now struck up 'Sons of

he Sea – bobbing up and down like this', though it must be said they played it rather ineptly since their recent work had been confined to rather more uptempo music in a much less martial style. At night they worked in the Tropicana Dance hall, Istanbul, as 'Billy Freeth's Big Band and Sheila.' (Sheila incidentally was the former Marine Band Master who'd saved up and had had the operation, and now blonded and hormoned into quite a pretty sight sang brightly frothy numbers with her former naval colleagues.)

The sun danced brightly on the bluey waters of the outer harbour, forty feet below the carrier's deck; and forty feet above the dancing waterline on the starboard side a temporary chute was hung, jutting out over the side. Down this the coffin would slide off the ship at forty-five degrees towards deep water, once it was wheeled across and placed upon the chute itself. At a given signal the chute would tip smartly up, and with a minimum of help, perhaps just a nudge from just a shoulder, the heavy coffin would begin to slide, to make its final exit in a steeply angled dive into the water end-side on. Thus the mechanics of the burial: gravity and grease.

At 2.45 the Chaplain led the officers of the carrier *Triumphant* in a procession to the brim of the enormous lift hole. They looked down into the darkness as slowly the lift-deck began to rise, bringing up the flagged oblong mound that was the last of Admiral Barrington.

Now the great crowd hushed, the Ministers of State fell silent, Commonwealth heads were bowed, and the Royal Prince stopped saying 'Wow' to Commander Gwen MacPherson's helpful notes on everything. At last solemnity broke out. Quietly the vast platform rose until it settled perfectly into the empty square of deck. The band struck up the hymn 'Nearer my God to Thee' and a thousand officers and men joined in.

'Nearer to Thee.' Dignity descended for the first time on that day. It is a strange thing but it happens at a funeral

The mournful hymn echoed round the harbour from the tannoys of the carrier. The tourists ceased their snapping to join in while locals looked impressed upon a British state occasion, witnessed the cirumstances of a thousand years of pomp.

'E'en though it be a cloud
That hideth Thee-e'

they sang feelingly, a collective mood upon them.

The hymn finished as the Chaplain stepped forward to the bier. 'Ashes to ashes, dust to dust' he began.

From his vantage point high in the superstructure of the carrier, Seaman Beal looked down on the superb display beneath: mathematically precise lines of officers and men in perfect ranks, sun gleaming on their whites; the VIP enclosure on the starboard side, whereE grouped behind the Royal Prince the Heads of State and Commonwealth Prime Ministers occupied the best view of the ceremony and of the final dispatch of the corpse. The foreign ambassadors stood just behind, the living diplomatic corps of Istanbul: the French, the Dutch, American, German, Swiss and Swedish (name them, for there's fifty-one or more), High Commisioners, Ambassadors, First Secretaries, Consul Generals, dignitaries of all descriptions, and forty different sorts of diplomat.

The Chaplain closed his book of prayers and started his address. The tannoy crackled with his voice.

'Admiral Barrington was a man.' Non-controversial

112

stuff he laid before them, and they listened as he painted scenes of happy Harrow schooldays, days of Civil Service in a distant land. Politely he praised the dead departed Minister of State, filleting his career from foreign fields to Foreign Secretary, omitting nothing but the flesh from his high-minded oratory. Gentle words for the dead, well-chosen and well-spoken.

'. . . his Commonwealth, his country and his Queen . . . let us pray.' At this command a thousand caps came off. 'Our Father' he led them.

'Our Father' they echoed obediently. The mumbled prayer ran round the ship.

'On earth as it is in Heaven.'

The 's's of the trespasses hissed in the sunlight. 'As we forgive them that trespass against us . . .'

Seamen Beal looked down upon a thousand lips moving together in prayer. The Power and the Glory.

'For ever and ever, Amen.'

'Caps on!'

A long silent pause.

Six sailors in full dress uniform stepped forward to the six brass handles, took the weight and heaved. The flag-draped coffin moved towards the ship's side, trundled on well-oiled wheels towards the chute.

A heavy silence. All eyes watched the slow movement of the flag. It reached the chute where, acting under muffled orders, the sailors heaved the heavy bier up and off the carriage on to the ramp itself. A simple tilt through forty-five degrees, and just a hint of push would send it off now.

A heavy drum roll and the white caps flashed in the sun again as they removed them for the National Athem.

'God save our Gracious Queen
Long live our Noble Queen . . . '

That's my Mum, thought the Royal Heir as he watched them singing lustily.

'Long to reign over us
God save my Mum,' he thought but didn't sing.

And now one little ceremony remaining before the forty feet of fall into the water. A dozen Marines, white spatted and uniformed in purple, discharged their rifles into the clear blue air. Crack! The sound echoed around the harbour, lifting birds from everywhere. The half a dozen seamen removed the flag and rolled it ceremoniously. There, underneath, the long dark polished oak gleamed. They started now to tilt the chute.

'Carrier salute!' A thousand hands flew to a thousand foreheads. The coffin started to edge forward.

'Blackmail bye-bye' thought Seaman Beal.

It was moving now, gathering speed, already off the ramp tipping downwards on its edge, falling, falling, falling, till it angled into the water with a diver's splash and shot rapidly beneath into the blue.

Nobody moved. Saluting, they remained firmly to attention, contemplating the patch of blue wherein the air-tight box had disappeared.

A minute passed. And another. Still they were loathe to move, their eyes drawn to the dancing reflections on the water. And then, just when the slightest ripple of a movement passed through their ranks – a gasp of disbelief – travelling with incredible speed the Admiral's coffin shot out of the water and climbed into the sky. Upwards, steeply it soared high, obeying the force that had sent it down.

> A solid oaken coffin
> As airtight as a tin,
> Nobody had bored the holes
> The sea could not get in.

Its journey through the sea had inscribed a perfect parabolic curve. Thrust forcefully in by the weight of its own fall it had plunged deeply down until gradually its travelling arc was levelled then it turned upwards as the rush and pressure of the sea increased upon the air tight tube, so that like a ball under water the sea pressed it ever faster upwards, rushing it and pushing at it while it gained momentum, till it popped out shooting up before the startled gaze of Istanbul and the thousand watchers on the ship.

Disbelief and pandemonium. The coffin had now reached the highest point and moment of its journey. For a split second it seemed to hover in the air until, fully forty feet out of the water, it gave in to the pull of gravity and twisting slightly in the sky it started to fall flatly for the sea whilst all looked on with fatal fascination. With a terrific smashing splat it landed broadside in the water. The force and angle of the fall had an effect upon the coffin as if it had been bounced on concrete. Something had to give. The coffin lid smashed open, and there before the horrified gaze of the mourners of all nations out fell the body of the Foreign Secretary and plopped into the sea.

Admiral Barrington's body, so long the subject of indignity, carted round the world from Cabinet to Commonwealth Meetings, photographed obscenely in an Istanbul hotel room, and now denied the final formality of a funeral, floated face down upon the water.

Aboard the carrier *Triumphant* nobody moved. Still saluting, the officers and crew awaited some order that would clarify the situation. The Admiral, uncooperative in death as he had been cooperative in life, steadfastly refused to sink. He floated in the water a few yards from where his now vacant coffin, filling swiftly up with water, disappeared beneath the surface without its former occupant.

Five minutes passed. Five uncomfortable minutes whilst they waited for the former Foreign Secretary's body to saturate and sink. But he was stuffed with all the mysteries of taxidermy and his form refused to fill with water.

A squeaking and a cranking rattle of chains indicated to the thunderstruck carrier that a boat was at last being lowered. The band struck up a tune.

'A life on the ocean waves' they played.

To the jaunty breezy Pompey melody the small boat gradually drew closer to the floating corpse of Admiral Barrington, and there, whilst the entire Commonwealth looked on embarrassed and aghast, the ratings in the boat stood up and prodded the stiff with their oars, trying to drive him under. But under water the Admiral would not go. Desperately they drove at him with paddles, pushed him heavily with the handles of their oars, beat him with boat-hooks, but still he would not sink. And so, to put an end to this fiasco, conducted before perhaps in all eight thousand pairs of eyes, they decided that he must be brought back to the ship for reburial in a different way. Now they tried to pull the Admiral's body into the small boat – no easy task this, since his clothes were ringing wet and holding water – and as they struggled and pulled away at his corpse to the breezy strains of 'A life on the ocean waves', the Bosun, stumbling backwards as the boat rocked violently, fell into the sea. A cheer went up from the shore, and then another as a rating fell in head-first after him.

There is a limit to what you can stand at a funeral, and slapstick is well beyond that limit. The two now in the water pushed away at the Admiral's feet, whilst the five remaining hauled hard at his head, so that with one heavy 'two-six-heave' the Admiral shot across them into the boat, scattering them like skittles and ending up on top of them in the main body of the craft.

The ratings rowed sheepishly towards the carrier *Triumphant*, wet, exhausted and embarrassed. As they reached the side of the ship a great undisciplined and uncalled-for cheer went up from a thousand uniformed throats. Commander Gwen MacPherson snorted, impotently furious, as the Royal Son and Heir beside him tittered. The Heads of State looked sideways as they smiled amongst themselves. Silly grins were everywhere.

'What a balls-up' said the PM.

The Arabs sat on the desert sand and stared at the platform stage, puzzling at the antics of the young British pilot officers in drag. Powdered, lipsticked and in makeshift parachute-silk dresses, the RAF had improvised superbly.

'Ladies and gentlemen' said the MC amidst hoots of glee at his wit, 'number forty-three on your song sheets, "The Sheik of Araby".'

Forty Arabs looked down at the meaningless hieroglyphics on the sheet on front of them whilst a hundred British voices sang.

'The Sheik of A-ra-by,
Itchycoo, itchycoo, itchycoo,
His love belongs to me,
Itchycoo, itchycoo, itchycoo. . . '

Underneath their feet the Number One tunnel stretched from below the centre of the platform stage to the hut twenty yards away. They'd had to go for the hut in the end since it was the only piece of cover for fifty miles. Mind you, a third of the Escape Committee (MacLeach, an alcoholic Scot, who'd once been in a British POW escape film) held out for tunneling the fifty miles, but in the end common sense prevailed for possibly the first time on the entire mission. The plan as conceived was a simple one: to reach the hut and radio their position. Like a lot of simple plans its beauty lay in its sheer impracticability. a) They didn't know who to radio, and *b*) they didn't know their position. Still it was better than doing nothing and it gave them an excuse for getting into drag.

'My dog's got no nose.'

'How does he smell?'

'Terrible' said an Arab in the front row.

At the other end of the tunnel, tension was mounting inside the hut. Sergeant R. E. Bates was wrestling with the tuner of an extremly old radio. So far they had managed to raise only the Arab's base in Ali and Victor Sylvester on the Overseas Programme. Neither was much use.

'For God's sake hurry, Bates' said the 2nd i/c to o/c commanding Raiding Party 1, Tunnel 1, code name 'Contact'. 'They're nearly up to the finale.'

'What's the hurry?' said Bates.

'I don't want to miss it. They're doing selections from *The Desert Song.*'

'Hello Britain' said Bates grandly, 'Hello Britain. This is the RAF. Is anybody listening?' A long pause. Apparently nobody was. 'Hello Britain. This is the RAF. Come in please.'

Another pause; and then surprisingly a little male North London voice: 'Hello? Is that the RAF? Over.'

'Yes, yes, thank God. Who are you?'

'Oh I'm Mr and Mrs Betty Pike, er, Number 14, Wizards End, Hemel Hempstead. It's part of the new housing estate, you know, just after you come out of the station, get a number 50, it'll take you right past the factory estate – we're just down the road, turn right over the bridge – you can't miss it. Where are you?'

'We are in Noman' said Bates, extremely clearly.

'Oh yes' said Mr Pike. 'What part of Gloucestershire is that exactly?'

'Now listen very carefully please.'

'Only I've never been to Gloucestershire, although my wife has a cousin who comes from up there herself and funnily enough we were only talking about her a year ago. "We must go and see your cousin Laetitia" I said to Betty – and she said, "Yes we must", but of course we never did.'

'Listen, please concentrate. We have an urgent message. This is most important.'

'Oh hang on, if it's important I'll get a pencil. Only I've got a terrible memory, everybody in our family always says so.' His voice continued faintly, mingled with another voice, a lady's, Mrs Pike's they presumed.

'Betty is that pencil by the telephone still?'

'Who is it dear?'

'It's the RAF.'

'What do they want?'

'They've got an urgent message.'

'Tell them to hurry up, its nearly "Z-Cars".'

'Righto. Hello? Are you still there RAF?'

'Yes, we are still here' said Sergeant Bates (R. E.) extremely clearly.

'Can you make your message short please as it's nearly time for "Z-Cars".'

'Yes, yes.'

'Not too short obviously. If it was too short there'd be no need to write it down.'

'Please listen for God's sake. This is the message. Message reads . . . '

'Shall I write "Message reads"?'

'No you can put that down later.'

'Oh. I'd better put it down now or I shall forget later. Right. There. Off you go.'

'RAF trapped in the desert on oil airfield in Noman. Captives of fifty hostile Arabs. Send help. God bless us all. Out. Did you get that? Hello. Oh my Gawd. Hello? Hello? Mr Pike?'

'Hello. Sorry about that RAF, the wife's cousin just arrived, Laetitia, you know the one I told you about, from Gloucestershire. Well talk about a coincidence, I was just telling her . . . '

'Shut up!'

'Excuse me. There's no need to adopt that tone, even if you are the RAF. I don't have to do this you know. I'm an amateur and I'm only in it for the fun I can get out of it.'

'I'm sorry' said Sergeant Bates, sweating heavily.

'That's all right. Point taken I trust.'

'Yes.'

'Good. Right, "Message reads. . . " Go on.'

'Didn't you get any of it?'

'No, fire away though – I'll get it.'

'RAF stuck in Noman desert with fifty Arabs. Send help urgently.'

'Oo, sounds quite exciting. What happens in the end?'

'What do you mean?'

'Do you get away, or do you all get killed?'

'We don't know, Mr Pike. Its not a play.'

'Oh. I thought it was an exercise.'

'No, Mr Pike. This is for real.'

'Ooo how exciting. Fancy this happening to me. Wait till the neighbours hear. I might get my picture in the Harpenden paper.'

'You certainly will. Now please Mr Pike, get that message through to London immediately.'

'Righto. Oh. Shall I take the A41 or shall I cut through on the B292 to the A1? It's quicker although I might catch the traffic.'

'Phone it through.'

'Oh yes. Where to?'

'Downing Street.'

'Oo. This *is* exciting. Er, one minute.'

'Yes?'

'Have you got the number? Hello? Hello RAF?

Oh dear, they've gone. Betty, put that kettle on, you'll never guess what . . . '

They certainly had gone. Quite distinctly up the tunnel the 2nd i/c on 'Contact' had heard the magic strains of *The Desert Song*. First things first. Now they heaved and breathed their slow way along the sandy tunnel towards the stage.

121

'Bags I'm Richard Attenborough on the way back' said Sergeant Bates.

On stage things weren't going too well. There had been an outraged murmur from their captors when they'd all come on in Arab robes. Many of the performers had not had time to change their female make-up and now they looked quite pretty in their blond bouffants and eyelashes. The Arab audience however, not understanding the language, thought that they were watching a satire on themselves – the implication of the satire being quite clearly that all Arabs are fairies.

Only Harish Hashish El Nordern prevented them from rising up in protest. He seemed to be enjoying the show – in fact he had laughed loudly, noisily and uncontrollably throughout. Now he was rockcng with laughter. One or two petulant glances from the stage greeted this outburst, they were doing the *Desert Song* bit straight. Fifteen drag Arabs advanced towards the front of the stage and started to sing. Harish Hashish howled. Another loud mutter of protest ran round the audience: no self-respecting Arab would sing like that. What were these British doing? The British were now linking arms and, worst of all, they broke into a dance.

Oh outrage! This was too much even though Harish Hashish El-Nordern had fallen off his stool with laughter. They sprang irately to their feet, waving their arms and shouting loudly. The music died, the dancing ceased, the cast stopped holding hands. The Arabs were extremely angry. The cast looked aprehensive; the Arabs ferocious. Now they were moving for the stage. The cast, eyes glinting in their mascara, stood by to repel the audience. It was like a disastrous first night. The Arab audience advanced slowly on the Arab actors. Confrontation. When suddenly –

'Hey look!' A great cry of alarm from the leading man. He was pointing out towards the desert to their right. Everybody stopped. Something was approaching in the strangest manner. You would have said that by its continual up and down movement it was ... bouncing. *Bounce! bounce!* It came closer, like a weary kangaroo, an exhausted survivor from their Suez mission bouncing its way back home. Yet now its leaps were weary and growing visibly smaller as it came. The bouncing bomb was near its end.

'Look out,' shouted someone, and everybody ducked. The Arabs too falling to the floor, although not knowing what this large black bouncing thing might be.

It was now within twenty feet of them and dropping straight towards the makeshift auditorium. There was a silence. It fell just two feet short and limped no higher than four feet over their heads to crash just clear of them beyond, where it rolled gently towards the hut. It limped up the one small stair, and disappeared inside the open door. There was a pause and then ... Whhhrrrrummphhhhh! The whole hut disappeared magnificently. The watching Arabs could not believe their eyes. They turned with admiration to the stage. Headfirst upwards through the stage trapdoor propelled at high speed by the blast, shot Sergeant Bates and 'Contact' squad. They landed in a sandy heap.

'Now,' said Squadron Leader Gimlet, 'Do you surrender or shall we have another one?'

Friday

Jonathan woke up with Number Nine, a headache and a feeling he should give up this sexist quest. The daughter of the Minister of Housing was an insipid bore. From the minute she'd surgically adjusted her cap, removed her face, dusted her crutch, sprayed her pits and asked him if he was ready for anything, he had felt his erection crumbling. She was as dull as he had thought. ('I've been married and everything, you really should try it – its terrible fun.') He managed to make it once and couldn't face the prospect of a repeat at any price. She'd watched him come – he doubted if she came, although she'd rolled her eyes a little and sighed politely at the time – and then as he had lain there, she said it. 'Super.' He winced. 'That was really super.'

Then hardly waiting for withdrawal, she'd jumped up off the bed and dashed away to douche. Toilette completed, pits firmly scrubbed again (for Christ's sake what had she done to make her sweat?) she bounced back into bed. Jonathan feigned sleep. But sleep did not come easily. He lay awake beside the tiny boring body and thought about it all. What was he doing wasting his time on this ridiculous quest? At twenty-five you're too old for political promiscuity. Nine tenths of the Cabinet. He'd got as far as Herrington in the twenties, but Herrington was only twenty-one when he first attempted to prise open the virginity of the tenth, though he was thirty before he finally gave up. Still, nowadays it's much easier. Why he'd hardly countered any resistance. It was only a matter of time, and what was the point of it? Who, nowadays, would be impressed? No, he was a fool to waste his time on sexual politics. 'I'm going to turn over a new leaf,' he thought, 'abandon all this chauvinism. In future I'm only going to fuck who I fancy.'

Big deal. Still, he felt the same way in the morning.

Unfortunately so did she.

Jim Sickert did a lot of thinking behind the back of the moon. He even talked aloud to himself since Houston couldn't hear him in those merciful forty-two minutes when he was loosed from their umbilical. 'It's your hand man' went his thinking. (He was a poker-playing man.) 'You've got the cards, you've got to call the odds. OK So they pay me the money. How do I collect? And even if I do collect, where can I go? Ten to one they'll quietly disappear me when I get back. That's what I'd do. They can't afford to let me loose because they can't afford to let the people know. Wait a minute! That's the angle, the people! That's it!'

When he emerged into the probing touch of radio contact, away from the silence of the moon's backside, he felt much better about raising Houston.

P I P: 'This is *Pelican*. Do you read me?'

P I P: '*Pelican*, this is Houston. Hi Jim.'

Just hear that phoney friendliness – boy had he got them worried.

P I P: 'I've changed my mind.'

The relief was apparent.

P I P: 'Glad to hear it Jim. We always knew you would.'
If they didn't always know it, seven years training in rigorous mind and body control that made a Jesuit College seem like a sunshine holiday home, would certainly have let them down badly. That a criminal mentality could slip through such a net. They had to believe he'd change his mind.

P I P: 'Yeah, you're right. I don't need that money.'

P I P P I P : 'Sure am glad to hear that Jim. This is Andy Scheist – wow did you have us worried for a while.'

P I P: 'This is Houston. Stand by *Pelican* for your orbital correction.' Business as usual. Jim Sickert stood by.

P I P: 'Oh there's just one thing Houston.'

P I P: 'What's that Jim?'

P I P: 'I want a job in the Administration.'

Silence in space. Static silence.

P I P: 'How's that again Jim?'

P I P: 'Just a job in the Administration,'

P I P: 'In government?'

P I P: 'Hey that's right.'

P I P: 'Hell Jim, we aren't politicians . . . '

P I P: 'You can fix it.'

P I P: 'It's a pretty tall order.'

P I P: 'You fix it; I'll pick them up.'

P I P: 'But Jim they've got to leave the moon within twelve hours.'

126

P I P: 'I know. Hey and listen. I want that offer from the President. And on television. Otherwise it's no go.'

P I P: 'Jim, now this is not the way democracy is run.'

P I P: 'With respect. You're wrong. You know it, and I know it, and it always will be, so long as *they* don't know it.'

P I P: 'Mission Control say they reluctantly accede to your requests. Stand by for correction figures.

P I P: 'Roger.'

He'd got them. They knew it and he knew it.

In Istanbul Seaman Beal gazed upon the debris of the previous evening. They'd had a bumper celebration night with fireworks and a display of glittering oriental nudes in tasteful poses, each one penetrated by a sailor in twelve different positions, representing the calendar months of the year. Each tableau had a tasteful verse accompaniment. Miss February was a tangle of legs and very athletic.

Miss March a merry masturbator
Accompanied by a large vibrator.

You get the idea. The whole act – or acts – took about an hour and a bit and both they and it were superbly mounted.

Enjoyable and educational were Seaman Beal's spectaculars. He had several other shows: 'The Seven Ages of Man,' 'The Seven Deadly Sins', 'The Four Nude Horsemen of the Apocalypse' (a quickie ten-minuter this for tourists) and the final grand concourse, 'A Tribute to Mr Heinz' or '57 Varieties', a moving tableau of all angles

127

and positions. But still, his favourite was the 'Months'. It had class.

The Prime Minister had not come, no doubt not trusting Seaman Beal, for had he not just luckily escaped the blackmail of the Foreign Secretary's photos? No, he stayed away, but better meat had come.

> 'HRH the Prince and Heir,
> Had never seen a lady bare.'

So, rhymed happily Seaman Beal that morning. He wrote all the link material himself – quite a turn of phrase. Oh he was in excellent spirits that morning after, was Seaman Beal. The sight of all that fornicating flesh had been too much even for a Royal British Prince, and he'd been taken quietly away and raped by Noreen, an exotic dancer from Birmingham. His face had been a happy daze; and happy days were here again, for Seaman Beal had filmed the Royal Command Performance in its amateur entirety. This precious reel of film was even now upon his desk.

'Careful my dear' he said to Mrs Birkenhead as she rubbed (she did for him daily).

'What is it?' said Mrs Birkenhead looking at the can of film.

'That,' said Seaman Beal, 'is my peerage.'

The PM walked unhappily through the corridors of the Gallipoli Hotel. 'Bobo,' he called out hopefully, 'Bobo?'

Beside him Splendiman, berated but surely not to blame for the blond youth's disappearance, helped him in the search. His concern was mainly for the Prime Minister, who even now was looking at him strangely as they walked.

'Bobo' said the Prime Minister. Where was the boy?

'The Queen's been phoning you again sir.'

'Damn the Queen.'

'I told her you were coming home today.'

'Good. Because I'm not.'

'Not sir?'

'Not until I find Bobo. Good God man, anything might have happened to him in this town.' And the P M shot Splendiman an accusing penetrating stare.

'Oh Gawd,' though Splendiman, 'he's still in love with me.'

Meanwhile the phone rang back in the powerful corridors of Downing Street's Number Ten.

'Jeffrey, there's a phone call through about the RAF.'

'Thank God. Where are they?'

'Apparently they're trapped in an oilfield in Gloucestershire by fifty Arabs.'

'I didn't know we had any oil in Gloucestershire. It's probably some nutter.'

'Name's Pike. Oh, yes and would you ring him back, he wants to know what happens in the end.'

The Truce of Noman's flight from Istanbul in the plane of the Royal Nomanese Air Force was delayed a little by his hangover. He had attended Seaman Beal's farewell pageant where he had also achieved a major private diplomatic coup with Vera from Gibraltar and Conchita from Solihull, but now the news of the RAF's incursion into his wilderness had made his departure for Ali, royal Noman capital, imperative.

Ali in Nomanese means 'oil' and 'the redeemer'. It must certainly have seemed that way to the most backward country of the world when excavations in the forties revealed that Noman was geographically the wrong way up. Its rich lands all lay beneath its sandy wastes.

Upon such a geographically significant though socially wasteful desert, trod the well worn bootees of the RAF. They marched on foot, escorted or escorting the forty Arabs – nobody was quite sure which – and they were Ali bound.

Squadron Leader Gimlet, till then the senior sane British Officer, had gone off his head again and now it fell to Sergeant Bates to guide them through the troubled land to the sparkling jewel of Ali, the oasis. Mind you, even the oases in the hardened Noman desert possessed their sour drawbacks, for they had filled up with oil, their water tarnished by the liquid gold. Oil may have brought wealth to Noman's land, but try telling that to a camel at a Nomanese watering hole.

So as the Truce's plane left Istanbul, a picture in the sun, and as the Truce said good morning to the Noman Royal Air Force – an Australian flyer called Bill – the RAF trudged slowly through the Truce's tiresome land.

At 10.15 a well organized group of heavily armed men snatched wages totalling a quarter of a million pounds from seven different branches of Barclays Bank simultaneously. The raid was planned with military precision. The vehicles in which they made their getaway were cleverly disguised as armoured scout-cars; the clothes they wore were cleverly similar to army patterns, with helmets, riot visors, and breathing masks to protect against tear gas, which cleverly resembled army patents. Even the arms they brandished – machine guns and automatic rifles– were cleverly disguised as army weapons. Some folks suggested that the army might be behind it.

Lady Candida had fallen in bed again. This time with a group she'd watched at Arabella's birthday ball. Afterwards she'd had them all. They'd played quite badly but they looked so pretty; with Candida it was lust at first sight. They were all from Eton and were called Note – that's Eton backwards, a musical accident, which is rather how their music sounded. They were a little shy of her supergroupie city ways, but Lady Candida ate her way through them willy-nilly. At first protesting at this form of cannibalism, for they were decent upright sort of lads, they came at last to see the merits of her mouth. Private Education is a wonderful thing.

Now she relaxed at their Honourable lead singer's Chelsea home and read the Morning *Times:* how some had been deported; some slain in war; some haunted by their wives; some sleeping killed. The lead singer of Note was the Honourable Simon Pyrrh (pronounced 'Purr' as in pussy – as in cat).

'Actually, would you like to come to the Albert Hall tomorrow?' He asked her Honourably in his Eton tongue.

'What that boring gig for the PM?' said Lady Candida, equally *au fait* with the political scene.

'Actually we're playing.'

'Are you really? I was supposed to be going with Arabella. I thought it was only a boring meeting.'

'Actually no, they're having a dance at the Dorchester afterwards. Actually its more of a ball really actually.'

Actually Simon always spoke like that.

'Might come' said Lady Candida. 'Depends what I've got on.'

And *who* one might say from her experience.

'Actually here's Mummy now.' The Honourable Simon left the room to Pyrrh all over Mummy who had spotted Candida already – in the way a bull spots a matador actually.

'Darling, please throw that filthy little slut out of here.'

'Actually Mummy she's not a slut.'

'She's a tart. I can tell. Why Candida hello, it's you. How nice to see you. How's your Father? Busy as ever? You know Norman always said that Chancellor was the most important job of all – purse strings of the nation and all that. You will stay to lunch won't you?'

Actually she wouldn't.

'Hello is that Your Royal Majesty? Damn. Hello Your Highness? Hi. Is there anybody there goddamit? Oh shit.'

'This is the Queen' said a voice in unarguable tones.

'Please state your business, your title and your name.'

'Oh hello there Ma'am, this is the President.'

'Not the Prime Minister?'

'No Ma'am, the President. . . of the United States of America.'

'Yes I remember you – you came to dinner with that funny man. We had lamb.'

'My Ambassador, yes Ma'am.'

'That's right. Have you got rid of him?'

'No, Ma'am.

'Good. He's extremely good value. Very funny man.'

'Thank you Ma'am. Fact is the reason I rang you, well, this might seem a little strange to ask, but, hell – have you ever done a movie?'

'Do you mean a motion picture?'

'I think I do Ma'am, yes, rightly so.'

'Only for the television. I had my own show you know. Of course there's the family bit at Christmas that the BBC do, oh, and we've done one or two spectactulars from Wales and so forth.'

'What I mean is Ma'am, would you care to be in a film? You see Warner Brothers will put up half the money if we can get . . . '

'A commercial motion picture?'

'Well yes Ma'am – naturally we'd hoped to get our money back at least. There's Omar Shariff . . . '

'Isn't he Egyptian?'

'He was Ma'am, yes, but now he's as American as the rest of us.'

'Mr President, the Queen of England does not appear in commercial motion pictures with Egyptians.'

'No, but . . . '

'Good day Mr President.'

'Royal motherfucker, she's hung up' thought the President undiplomatically. 'Women. There's just no trusting them.' And then they told him that the spacemen were in trouble. A serious technical difficulty which threatened all their lives.

'Great!' said the President. 'A crisis at last. That's the first good thing that's happened today. Now we can get the public right behind us.' He even left the bathroom.

At the moment that the Yanks pulled out of Cambridge for South-East Asia (via Bletchley, Nuneaton, Rugby Midland and Liverpool) General Atkinson was staring miserably at a map. It was a large and detailed cartographic work entirely covered now by a mass of squiggles, dots and lines and marks. This was the area they had searched and bombed and blasted for three days, without success. Never mind a needle, they couldn't even find the haystack. The fifty volunteers had disappeared into thin air. Commie bastards. 'You can't trust anyone nowadays' thought General Atkinson as his replacements started off from Cambridge, England, and his replacement from Cambridge, Massachusets.

The British Navy meanwhile was steaming hard towards the Bosphorous. All communications lost, she was tarnation bent for Istanbul come hell or high water. And therein lies a warning. For at high water the Dardanelles is just a narrow channel, but at low water this distance is considerably lessened; in fact two thinnish ships might only just scrape past.

The Russian navy, at this time at anchor in the Sea of Marmara, heard vague reports about the British Suez mission, and having nothing else to do swiftly put to sea, heading for the Aegean and the Med. The American fleet whose task it was to follow and be followed by the Russian navy, watched its charge weigh anchor and sensing something might be up – and anyway having nothing else to do – straightway gave chase. Gradually overhauling the Russian fleet she was pursuing, the Americans drew level by the time they reached the narrow entrance to the Dardanelles, where neither would give way. Strictly speaking, by the ordinary rules of the sea the foremost vessel should be allowed to pass and go ahead along the right hand channel, but there were various complicated considerations of international maritime navigation and the simple insurmountable complication that neither Admiral of the Fleet would give way. The two fleets therefore churned along side by side towards the narrow passage of the Dardanelles, which at that very time had low tide. There was considerable doubt that they would fit between the 'nelles' historic flanks but by ill judgement and good luck they managed it. Complete with angry signals of all sorts, and tedious recriminations back and forth, the two fleets slid in safely, closely, cheek to cheek, with just a narrow strip of water in between.

Imagine then the English Admiral's view from the Aegean end of that narrow channel. All radio communications lost, he nevertheless had a clear visual sighting of two enormous fleets steaming straight towards him, towards the very spot his own fleet was rapidly approaching. His flagship now was half a mile from them. Should he come about? Vice-Admiral Haugh looked briefly at his orders – MOSTURGENTWARDS

ISTANBULWARDSMUSTGOTOWARDS – and then briefly at his fleet in line astern; then searching through his glasses he scanned the narrow piece of sea between the fast-approaching fleets.

'Stand by to come about' spoke up Commander Beste-Welcome, anticipating.

'No sir' said the Vice-Admiral Haugh. 'The British Navy will not come about. If we turn now they'll hit our fleet amidships, we would not stand a chance. No, Commander Beste-Welcome, we're going in. There's just a groat of sea between them, a gnat's bollocks worth between their fleets – we'll plumb right up the middle. It's the Nelson touch.'

So plumb they did, to the amazed and startled eyes of the American and Russian fleets, both furiously dispatching signals which the Admiral's smashed communications room ignored. Yet neither of their fleets could do a thing: they could not back up; they could not turn; they could hardly run aground and concertina their entire fleet behind them. They had to keep coming steadily on, head on, towards the British navy.

Collision seemed inevitable and all eyes on the first three ships were closed as the yards narrowed down to twenty and then ten. It seemed there must not be room enough between, and yet when all eyes opened again the British ship *Return* was seen to lead the British column by a hair's breadth through the moving walls of steel. Americans to the left of them, Russians to the right; on either side irate sailors yelled abuse in several languages at the British ship as she squeezed tight between.

'By Jove, we've got them sore' chortled Vice-Admiral Haugh.

And sore they were. Yet there were definitely inches to spare between the mighty fleets, as steadily but sedately they passed in three long lines astern for twenty minutes at dead slow, two in one way, one in t'other. Twenty minutes steaming with nothing but an inch or two between them and disaster, until finally the British flagship rapidly approached the last ships in the opposing lines. *Return* was only seconds from clear water, and just about to break quite free from the tight constrictions of this moving corridor of steel, when disaster, for so long courted, was finally married.

One of the three master mariners – all three denied it vigorously later – coughed, perhaps with relief, perhaps with a cold. A cough is not a criminal offence, and yet what an effect it had upon the length and breadth of those three columns. The small gap closed. The foremost British ship stuck fast between the rearmost two of the adjacent fleets, tight, bound, wedged, secure. The effect of this upon the British fleet was catastrophic. One by one they ploughed gently into the rear of the vessel that they were following, so that the British fleet became a single length of solid steel for nearly two miles.

The rearmost British ship *Labia Major*, a destroyer, spotted early the escalating pile-up of the fleet, and trying hard to stop within the distance went off course. Attempting vainly to avoid the Russian fleet, she bounced into the Yankee boat ahead and wedged tight between the two, blocking their exit entirely. No one could get in or out. There was such a sudden shaking of ships from side to side, such a running of vessels aground, such a wedging, and a squeezing of all ships tight, that within ten minutes of that first and fatal cough the entire three fleets were sealed up solid within the narrow passage of the Dardanelles. Wedged together for nearly two miles, the most sophisticated navies in the world were welded into one long traffic jam that cut the Black Sea from the Med, and sealed up Istanbul into an inland harbourage. Lloyds underwriters raced each other for the highest windows at the news.

The Nelson touch indeed.

'Hi Jim, this is the President.'

'Hello Mr President. Gee sure is nice to hear your voice up here.' (Give them the works Jimmy boy, the full schmaltz; they're listening in from coast to coast.)

'I sure am sorry to hear about your difficulty, Jim' said the President.

Houston had written this bit. In their story, Jim's mothership, *Pelican,* had developed a serious and mysterious fault. Instead of taking himself home and leaving the others to their certain deaths, he was bravely staying there to risk his life in an attempt to pick them up. It was a really beautiful plot that Hollywood would not have bettered. Houston now believed its own simulators. They'd pioneered the new fact/fiction programming for all eventualities and now they simply used an artificial programmed emergency eventuality (APE) as cover for their real story. The APE was now released amongst its brothers in the press.

PIP: 'Hell Mr President, its nothing we can't handle.

138

Why if you had the number of people helping you that I have, you'd have no problems too.'

P I P: 'That's really very humble of you to say that Jim, because we know and all America knows the risk you're taking for those boys on the moon.'

P I P: 'Thank you Mr President.'

P I P: 'And Jim I've spoken to a little lady you know quite well; I mean your wife Jim.'

P I P: 'Tell her I ain't washing up too well here.' (Oh America how you loved that.)

P I P: 'Ha ha.' (The President laughed at *me*!) 'I guess you won't have to wash up if you'd accept my invitation to dine with me at the White House Jim. Dotty and I would sure like it if you and Jane would come over and eat.'

(Jane was being eaten by the *Time* reporter's mouth. Boy did he have a story now; he could afford to keep her happy. 'Oh my God, Jim,' she thought, 'what will I wear.' She was naked.)

P I P: 'That would be an honour Mr President.'

P I P: 'Then it's a date.'

P I P: 'If it's OK with Houston sir.'

P I P: 'Oh I think we can persuade your boss to let you go.' (A laugh for the President. He liked people who fed him lines.) 'Hnuh, hnuh' he went, unpleasantly simulating laughter. 'Oh and one other thing Jim. I've asked the Senate and their wives to be there, and all the heads of American Industry and their wives and all the astronauts . . . ' (not their wives, thought Jane happily, runnily) '. . . because Jim I want you to accept a job in my Administration.'

He said it, he said it, he said it, and all America heard him.

'Gosh,' thought the *Times* reporter, 'I'm finally licking the Administration . . .'

P I P: 'Gee Mr President it's nice to know that someone has such confidence in me. I only hope that Andy and Dick have as much faith in me.'

You know what Dick and Andy thought.

P I P: 'Well good luck my boy.'

P I P: 'Thank you Mr President. Please tell the folks back home that I'm going to do everything I possibly can to get my friends up off that moon. That's my primary concern. If I can manage that I think working for you might come as a relief.'

P I P: 'Then it's a deal' said the President.

P I P: 'It certainly is' said Jim Sickert.

P I P P I P:

Andy and Dick in one sixth gravity listened, impotently furious. Television trebled its rating every minute as more and more people heard. Word went round the presses of the world: A C C I D E N T. Immediately all work ceased and sets went on: the living theatre tonight presents Jim Sickert in 'The Crippled Ship' or 'How to put your friends before your life'.

Cool crop-haired NASA technicians listened to the exchange in silence. They showed no emotion. Perhaps they felt none. (Would a computer have a crew-cut?) They almost believed the drama which they had created. From now on they simply had two missions: the real one, a comparatively 'easy' moon orbitual rendezvous; and the television one, the drama of a space link-up with a desperately crippled mother ship.

High above, on coast to coast TV, Jim Sickert bravely smiled his little craft through the yawning credibility gap.

Watching him on the screen over the curly head of the *Time* reporter, his near-orgasmic wife had a sudden vision of the entire White House Press Corps with their tongues hanging out.

The Prime Minister had not stirred; for three hours he had stayed within his room. Already they had missed one flight, but no, he would not leave without Bobo. All sweaty afternoon they'd searched the seamy streets of Istanbul, the rather tubby form of the PM plodding pallidly round the shabby streets forlornly shouting 'Bo-bo, Bo-bo' as one hails a missing cat. All in vain. Then desperation slid into despair inside the peeling bedrooms of the Gallipoli Hotel.

Splendiman, apparently in charge, feared for his job. What a predicament. He dared not leave the PM alone, and yet he hardly dared face him in his room, not for his insults, but his advances. 'I must be careful if it's me he's fallen in love with' he reasoned. So, wisely, after several hours prevarication, he sent for Seaman Beal – the eyes and ears and private parts of Istanbul.

Beal knew at once of course. In fact he was surprised and angry with himself for not divining who it was young Bobo had actually been with. Of course, the PM! Everything then fitted. How could he have considered it was that buffoon Splendiman. Now, damn it all, he had no photographic evidence on which to stake a modest claim. Even the snap of Bobo naked, the PM had wrested from him – to give it to the Secret Service! Yes he'd been thoroughly given the run around by the little bent PM. How could he have suspected Splendiman o. keeping a fancy man on his money? He listened now to that man's circumlocutious explanations and saw it all Well for the good of England – and since he could think o. no way he might turn a buck from how the hanc stood now – he must break it gently to the grieving lover.

'I'm afraid' said Seaman Beal 'that Bobo has left Istan-bul.'

The Prime Minister nodded. 'Alone?' he asked.

Seaman Beal looked mutely to Splendiman for help Splendiman looked away. 'No sir. I'm afraid not.'

'Then who's he with?'

'Well sir . . .'

'Dammit man, who is Bobo with?'

'The Truce sir.'

'The Truce of Noman!'

'Yes sir.'

'By God, the crocodile!'

'I think you may misunderstand his motive sir.'

'I don't think I do' said the distraught deserted, dream-ing of his loved one's rounded form. 'Running off with Bobo while dissembling as a friend.'

'Precisely because he is your friend' said Seaman Beal If I may explain.'

'Explain what you want' said the PM petulantly.

'The thing is sir, when you made Splendiman and Bobo change their rooms, they moved your Bobo out and pu him in another double.'

'With the Truce?'

'Unfortunately the hotel was extremely overbooked

and they thought since he was already sharing Bobo wouldn't mind.'

'Oh my God, then that explains it.'

'Not quite. You see the reason that the Truce himself was so friendly and so helpful to you . . . '

'Yes?'

'Was because of your gift to him.'

'What gift?'

'In many African states it is the highest compliment to a friend to exchange a gift of . . . '

'Of what!'

'Of wives.'

'Wives!'

'The Truce believed you'd sent him Bobo as a token of respect.'

'Then he's not bent' said Splendiman aloud to his own horror.

'No, he is not . . . left-handed,' said Seaman Beal reproachfully, 'but he is too polite a man to return a gift once proffered.'

'Oh God' said the PM.

'They left this morning for Noman' said Seaman Beal. 'Incidentally Prime Minister, did you know that's where the RAF are?'

Saturday

Jonathan woke up alone. Behind his bed the number nine remained as evidence that his resolution had not faltered, and beside his bed – corroborating evidence – a note from Number Six (Pollution's daughter) to say she was no longer polluted and he could have her properly, lay totally unanswered.

He felt better for his new leaf, even virtuous, a feeling that he had not felt for years. No longer would he need his season ticket for the Special Clinic, the bright blue card that indexed all his errors – a season ticket of such similar design that it had once gained him entrance to the Chelsea Ground for a Cup-tie.

Yes he was definitely feeling satisfied with himself when his heart leapt at the sound of the doorbell. Ah, he thought, you've been so good you deserve a lay. But it was only Cecil.

'Hello. What on earth are you doing here?' Cecil's long face looked mournfully up at him. 'Come on in.'

'Yes, alright then. I say what a grotty flat.'

'Thank you' said Jonathan. 'Would you like some coffee?'

'Mm, rather' said Cecil settling.

'What can I do for you then?'

'Well it's like this . . .'

'Oh dear' said Jonathan.

'Don't be beastly till you've heard. A dear friend of mine has gone and killed herself.'

'How careless all your friends are. You should give up chasing foxes. Its unforgivable how you keep killing ourselves; we'll soon have no aristocracy left at all.'

'Oh do shut up. I knew I shouldn't have come. The thing is she wasn't killed *à la chasse* at all.'

'Oh.'

'No. Automobile accident.'

'Where?'

'In Knightsbridge.'

'Knightsbridge? Was she walking?'

'No driving.'

'Whereabouts?'

'The multi-storey car park.'

'Outside.'

'Inside.'

Jonathan turned to make the coffee.

'How can anybody kill themselves *inside* a multi-storey car park?'

'She was a lovely girl. Absolutely fiendish driver. Still she was extremely nice. You should meet her.'

'I probably will.'

'No, I mean you should have met her.'

'Yes, I'd have liked to.'

'Would you really!' said Cecil brightening 'because . . .' he paused, 'I've brought the next best thing.'

'You haven't brought her!' said Jonathan, too late as from beneath his coat Cecil produced another hideous casket designed by someone to deter cremation.

'There she is.'

'Cecil this is too much.'

'I only want your help. You see she used to positively adore the Proms and she desperately wanted, when she went, to have her ashes scattered . . .'

'Not the Albert Hall!' said Jonathan.

'Yes,' said Cecil, 'and as the Police are on to me – I have a record and everything . . .'

'Oh no' said Jonathan firmly.

'I'd only ask you to take her in.'

'I'm not scattering your friends.'

'Just to take her past the doorman. I'll meet you inside.'

Jonathan hesitated. 'Promise?'

'Yes honestly Jonathan.'

'All right, but if you let me down, I warn you I'll dump her in the nearest waste paper basket.'

'Jonathan! She was related to Royalty. You wouldn't put her in a litter bin?'

'Well if you don't meet me Cecil I'll leave her in the Gents.'

Admiral Barrington's body flew into London's Heathrow at ten that morning, with the help of British Airways. Not first class this time, alas, nor tourist like the PM now. No, they'd conned the aircraft company by insisting that the Admiral's coffin went as hand luggage, and being as how it was the Government involved and they could easily sell them all off into private hands, the aircraft company had complied. The Admiral's coffin therefore – his second in two days – now had a reddish label tied to a brass handle designating his remains as cabin baggage.

The PM picked with his plastic knife at his plastic food and wished he too was travelling baggage. He was extraordinarily upset. He spoke not a word to Splendiman on the flight and ignored the awful nudgings of the British trippers next to him. He began to smoke on take-off and steadfastly refused to buckle up his seat belt, alarmingly individualistic tendencies brought on by his grief for the absent Bobo, Britain's gift to Noman's leader. In this mood Jeffrey found him, at last, the late Prime Minister and his even later cabin baggage.

'Hello PM! My word you do look well.' Jeffrey lied.

'I told you it was him' said a nudging Northern voice. 'What did I tell you? I knew it were PM.'

'Christ Almighty' said it's friend, 'God help us.'

It was traditionally raining as they stepped into the hired Humber, dodging comments from the press.

'Just print the usual things' said Jeffrey on a lobby basis.

That Saturday morning the Gay Liberation Front attacked. Suburban warfare. A carefully worked out infiltration of the suburbs, goosing shoppers, manhandling husbands' walking dogs, and everywhere molesting males. There were sit-ins in lingerie shops, kiss-ins in kitchenware, group-gropes in grocers, suck-ins in supermarkets and buggery in butchers' shops. A carefully conceived plan to shock the public into recognition of equal rights. Esher to Purley was a battlefield of outraged propriety; Surbiton lay stunned; Walton-on-Thames would never quite recover. It was a field day for the oppressed repressed; a nightmare world of nastiness for normals. In suburb after suburb they fought hand to hand, wrist to wrist, against the gay marauding hordes: chaos was everywhere. It was worse than Hampstead Heath on New Year's Eve. In Stevenage alone there were 144 cases of gross indecency.

The Cabinet met at two and briefly welcomed home their leader. He sat unmoving, lost in thought, whilst they, relieved of his interest, sifted through a pile of backlogged business. They hurried through more political decisions in ten minutes with the PM back than many governments in a lifetime. They were like a private board on the brink of bankruptcy (which in a way they were). Any decisions might help.

The Tate Gallery, they confirmed could go to America; the price was right, an export licence would be granted. This gave them bags of cash in hand to move on to the second motion of the day – the cancellation of the *White Elephant*. Yes, they decided suddenly, let's be rid of it and of the French. We owe the beastly Frog a good stab in the back they argued, and this would make him furious, while killing off a national debt. In any case the bloody double-barrelled thing would never fly economically. As a compromise they would keep the airport in Berkshire.

Let that still be built at least as a sop to the expansionists, or else the Minister for Pollution would have no option but to resign. Yes, keep the airport but cancel the plane that made it necessary.

They'd got the bit between their teeth this Cabinet. They'd found a taste for making quick decisions and they pandered to it wonderfully, indulgently: approving schemes, voting money, cancelling contracts, on and on they went. Hyde Park could, yes, become a golf course for the Hilton, if the price was right; medicine should be made more expensive to deter illness; football could and should be taxed; railways must and ought and would be handed back to private enterprise. No, they would not help the large industrial concern which had appointed a receiver. No matter that ten thousand men would lose their jobs, the economy could stand ten per cent unemployment – it encouraged healthy growth. Yes, the Civil Service should be run entirely by the private sector, so too should telephones, and sewage ought to be in private hands. Yet they would not hive off the best bits of the army, though they felt severely tempted. The country was not ready for a private enterprise army. (Soon baby.) Besides, there were loud rumours that these bank raids were army planned and executed. The raiders had escaped to Ireland in suspiciously army-looking helicopters and were last seen entering what looked amazingly like a British army barracks. But all this was mainly heresay evidence from a mass of independent eyewitnesses, and an 'independent' tribunal would probably ignore it.

Still, it does explain how, whilst all other publicly owned properties and companies were being split up amongst the party faithful, the army came to be left out.

'It's much better than giving peerages' said Pollution happily, as his uncle received a major slice of British Cake.

To all the frenzied Cabinet activity, the Prime Minister said not a word. Motionless he sat amongst them like their recent Foreign Secretary. Though his body was not yet stuffed and stiff, his mind was in a foreign land. He pictured Bobo in a Noman harem surrounded by enormous black eunuchs. Unless Bobo himself had been . . . no, perish the thought; the Truce would never do that, not to Bobo's little nadgers. I only hope he's happy, thought the desolate Prime Minister.

The PM heard them ramble on, thought he heard them suggest some minor hanging legislation, heard them talk of flogging students but couldn't tell whether they meant beating or selling or he might have dreamt it; in any case they looked quite busy. He nodded his approval to their choice of Foreign Secretary, some friend of theirs from Industry, a chap called Pyrrh. He would do quite as well as anyone, and certainly much better than the dead one that they'd had for months. Yes, yes, they could if they liked require coloured people born in Britain to register with the police, providing it was for their own good and not at all a racist policy. Yes, everyone ought to be encouraged to go home where they had come from, even if it was their grandfather's home and they had never been there. What was it all to do with him, without his precious Bobo?

At about three thirty Jeffrey came in and woke the PM from his second reverie that day.

'A couple of phone messages sir.'

'Oh.'

Jeffrey bent down and whispered in his ear. The Cabinet strained hard to listen, but the Home Secretary was droning on about deporting all the troublesome Irish out of Ireland and they did not catch what Jeffrey said.

'Lord Bishop phoned.'

'Do I know him?'

'Bobo's father.'

'Oh dear. What did you say?'

'I stalled him, but I think he thinks there's something up.'

'Oh.'

'The other thing is sir, the Queen telephoned.'

'Jeffrey, she's been pestering me all week.'

'I feel you ought to know sir, she gave me a message. She's decided to emigrate.'

'What?'

'Her and the whole family. They're pissing off to Australia.'

'Bloody heck.'

'She says she's fed up with this bloody country so she's going down under where they appreciate Royalty.'

'The damn cheek.'

'Absolutely sir. They're all off. The whole bloody tribe. Assisted passage.'

'What shall we do Jeffrey?'

'Blackmail the Australians to refuse her entry! Stop the cricket tour and all that?'

'No, would never work – nobody cares about cricket any more. Shall we have any Royals left?'

'Oh yes, plenty of minor ones I expect.'

'But no direct line.'

'No sir.'

Pity Bobo isn't here, thought the PM, wristfully.

Aboard the mother ship *Pelican,* Jim Sickert opened the narrow hatch that separated him from the newly-docked lunar module. (The world had held its breath. W O R L D H O L D S B R E A T H, said the headlines everywhere.) The hatch swung open and through it came the two lunarnauts, Andy Scheist and Richard Grabowsky.

'Hi boys' said Jim cheerfully.

Not a sound in return. Their eyes avoided his. He might as well have *been* in Coventry.

'Well I'm sorry you're taking it like this' said Jim pleasantly. 'I feel you ought to be a little more cooperative – why I've just saved your life on TV. You should hear what they're saying about me. It makes a guy feel real humble.'

P I P : '*Pelican* this is Houston.'

P I P : '*Pelican.* Astronauts safely aboard. Boy they're in great shape. My what a wild reunion we're having. I guess I'm too embarrassed to tell you what they've been saying about me.'

P I P : (Houston could guess) 'Roger. Oh we have the President for you Sickert.'

'This is better than the Normandy film' thought the President. 'Screw Warner Brothers, I've got the rights on this spectacular. This boy's bigger box-office than Omar Sharif.'

While they returned to earth in silence – two days of purely technical communication (that's easy for an astronaut) – Jim Sickert became a national hero. In America only his name of all three astronauts was now remembered; only his deed of staying with his crippled ship to save them was recalled. All America fell in love with Jim Sickert and his myth: he was their boy, he'd been a good American, humble, honest and brave. They left off their adoration of a junior officer who'd single-handedly wiped out two villagefuls of Asian civilians, and worshipped only Jim. Demonstrations of affection broke out everywhere. He received the freedom of the City of Baltimore; Norman Mailer invited him to dinner; television wet it's pants for him. He was a hero.

On the second day of his silent return the President increased his offer via the telephonic link at Houston. Another major space first.

Sadly Vice-President Bugle lowered the eighteen Old Glory flags in his official residence; sadly he unscrewed his patriotic shower attachment; sadly he packed his all-American golf clubs and returned to the oblivion from whence he'd come. Jim Sickert was the new Vice-President.

What a scoop for the *Time* reporter who'd stuck so steadily to his job on Mrs Jane.

'Ball me again' said Mrs Sickert. 'I'm the VP's wife.' Power is a wonderful thing. 'Hey, just be delicate about it' said Mrs Jane. 'You're screwing someone who's just a heart's beat away from being First Lady.'

The RAF was still marching wearily across the great white sands towards the Noman capital of Ali. Another day and they would be there, and not a word from England. Corporal Ponson, the latest senior sane British officer, led them fearlessly onwards into the heat of the early evening.

The navy for their part were still stuck fast within the confines of the Dardanelles. The three fleets, thus unwillingly wedged together, now formed the largest, widest, longest bridge in the world. Not one of the three fleets was talking to the others. It was quite some bridge.

In Ireland the army was experiencing one of the largest share-outs since Attila. Wages were pretty high that week, but still they'd left sufficient in the kitty to defray future expenses. They had a long way yet to go before they would have enough to let them pay to move the army out of Ireland and away from blasted petrol bombs. They'd found their place in the sun, had the army. Near Bermuda, that's where they were going, at their own expense, away from the quarrelsome Irish – when they'd made enough, of course.

In South-East Asia, a group of fifty well armed, politically educated liberators who had escaped destruction by a large American force till lately commanded by a General Atkinson (now Mr Atkinson of Detroit Motors), swept into the fertile farmlands of Malaya to be hailed by the people as revolutionary heroes. CIA educated they set to work constructing a collective socialist state with all that the Americans had taught them. So this was the Domino Theory.

The Albert Hall was bathed in flood-light. Television vans surrounded it; gaudy yellow for Commercial, khaki drill the BBC, linked up with their snaky thick black umbilicals. Quite a crowd were out, attracted by the magic of big names: the first-night gawpers come to stare at Royalty and the cinematic wonders of the day. They stood about in little groups waiting for the faces they could recognize, determined not to be impressed. ('She's that much fatter in the flesh.') Yet despite themselves, they could not fail to be impressed by this most impressive of affairs. Sycophantic starlets from the world of cinema were there to bring some glamour to the victory occasion. Little short fat heads of studios, with their younglet wives all teeth and cleavage for the press of cameras; directors who were failed writers, or failed actors, or simply failed directors; fags of all nations; professional alcoholics, second cousins to the press; lobby correspondents with their smug handouts for a mind; society dentists who did the teeth of such and such when so and so had punched them out; society hairdressers, there because they knew too much; and society columnists, because they knew too little. Society, firmly represented by a wealth of tradesmen, tailors, trichologists, restaurateurs, hip accountants, whores of all sexes, actors, starlets, and comedians: they all bustled their self-important way into the fifty-guinea bean-feast – the Albert Hall – for speeches and awards, and afterwards they would all ball at the Dorchester.

Jonathan, suffering the indignity of what is called 'correct attire', surveyed the goggling crowd with alarm. Under his arm the casket felt enormous – they were bound to spot it. Clutching Cecil's friend's remains beneath his coat and holding in a trembling hand the large gilt invitation, supplied by courtesy of Cecil's friends (royalty welcome free, half price for peers), Jonathan pushed his way between the oohing and the aahing onlookers.

'Who's that then?' said the crowd as he elbowed his way through to the red carpet.

'That's nobody' they told him, scornfully rebuking him for being just like them.

Jonathan need not have bothered worrying about the casket. The doormen there were so intent on keeping out the crowd and fighting off their continual attempts to squeeze inside, that anyone with a bomb could easily have walked straight in, providing that he waved an invitation. Jonathan waved his invitation and passed amongst the privileged. He wasn't sure what to do – Cecil's plan was typically vague – and so he stood for quite ten minutes in the hallway as the flash-lights popped, wondering whether Cecil had got in, till finally it occured to him that the most likely place was at his table. He went inside between the floral tributes and the frenzied fronds of hanging green things. The place looked and felt like a hot house run by a gardener with green fingers and bad taste. The central rostrum of the Hall was carpeted and flowered in a riot of clash. There was a podium and a white-draped table, which was fully laid for fourteen, a superfluous touch this since there were no kitchens on the premises and no one would get fed. Apparently it added to the effect. Around the pit many more tables had been set as though it were a night-club or a banqueting hall. Indeed each proudly sported a virgin bottle of champagne – champagne which on closer inspection resembled soda pop, which in fact it was: an inspired piece of 'dressing' by the television wallahs. It gave the gathering class without additional cost.

Each table had its number and its floral attribute which corresponded to the number and flower on the gilded invitation card. Jonathan, detesting gladioli which his invitation designated, eventually found his table via the number, noticing with dismay that it was large and already occupied. He needn't have worried, for the occupants utterly ignored him when he squeezed between them into a vacant chair at the far end. Occasionally they glanced at him while they conversed as though he were a painting or a view.

Opposite him a professionally ugly girl of anything between eighteen and thirty-five had tried to improve on nature's unkind gift of face with a disastrous hair-do and a gouache touch of pancake make-up. She had achieved the startling effect of emphasising every ill-conceived contour.

' 'Ello' she said very suddenly to Jonathan, in horrid Kensington, as if at last deciding that he was alive.

'Hello' said Jonathan carefully.

'With Cecil?'

'Yes.'

'Good chap.'

Jonathan was just deciding whether he or Cecil was the good chap she'd referred to when an extremely nice body squeezed past him. Its occupant had a smiling face, perhaps a little vacuous, and a pronounced giggle. The huge one opposite him tried to pretend the body was not there; Jonathan couldn't. He turned and smiled and looked up at it, but got no further than the breasts which were indeed at his eye level. The nipples were quite frankly pointing at him through the thin crepe material. It took him a minute to speak.

'Can I help you?' he said, putting himself completely outside the large one's scheme of reference.

'Mm I expect so.' The voice was surprisingly Kensington, though the look was firmly Fulham Road.

'Hello' said Cecil, interposing his body in a Lytton Strachey kind of way between Jonathan and the pretty one. The pointed nipples followed their owner and flopped into a chair beside him.

'I can no further go' she said by way of introduction and stared happily and dreamily into the middle distance.

'High as a kite' thought Jonathan.

'Have you brought my friend' said Cecil, never a stander upon ceremonies. Jonathan brought forth the casket. The huge one opposite widened her eyes, a disastrous mistake.

'Well must dash' said Cecil. 'Sorry to be such a bore. See you at the ball.' Casket under arm he sauntered off.

'What's he got there?' said the large one sharply.

'It's a bomb' said Jonathan confidentially.

'Strange fellow' she confided. 'But he's a pet.'

'Anybody's a pet compared to you' thought Jonathan, smiling nicely at her.

The lights in the Hall dimmed suddenly, a British hint this, which leaves a wake of tripping, pushing, scrambling late-comers falling over one another blindly in the aisles. Testy usherettes, who seemed not to do their job for money but out of some deep favour to the audience, rudely shouted their curt instructions in that particularly irritating voice reserved for their profession. A titter of clapping which grew into polite applause greeted the sight of a line of blinking nervous people stepping up into the strong lights. A hush fell. A small moment of embarrassment while those inside the pool of light hovered around their place cards; a slight feeling of musical chairs whilst they changed places; and then they were all seated.

Jonathan, from the security of his table end, looked round the packed hall. Really they were quite cut off, him, the large one and the body. Cosy. The body might have noticed this herself for as the lights went down she leaned towards him, and now he sniffed her musty perfume whilst she moved her exquisite half-naked frame against his side and snuggled up. She was quite gone.

'Penguins' she giggled.

'Nipples' he replied, not wishing to seem out of it. The body seemed to find his words deeply and significantly amusing. The large one in front of them noisily scraped her chair around to face the stage, giving them the full benefit of her back, which was indeed considerate. The Home Secretary had risen.

'My lords, ladies and gentlemen' he began. The Hall echoed. 'We are gathered here tonight on this gala occasion, to pay tribute . . .'

Jonathan stopped listening. A hand had reached across and settled firmly on his crutch. He dismissed the wild idea that it was the large one and noted with surprise that the body next to him knew what she was about. He edged his chair close in to the table so that his crutch and the hand that even now was unzipping his hired flies were hidden from casual view. She was soon into his underpants and playing with him deftly between her expert fingers. He looked about him in the dark; all eyes were on the stage. 'If rape is inevitable . . .' thought Jonathan, lying back to enjoy the speech.

The Home Secretary was enjoying himself too. A captive audience was what he liked the most; indeed he spent a lot of his time lecturing to prisoners. He spoke now to these favoured few about Istanbul, speaking from rough notes of Jeffrey's which he had polished into clichés. At his side the PM palely sat, staring glumly at the tablecloth with thoughts of Istanbul and Bobo. From his pocket he produced Seaman Beal's splended portrait of the boy, bollock-naked in the Istanbul hotel room. Splendiman had been removed from the artistic print. Two small tears started as he gazed upon the blond-haired youth, now the property of the Truce – a present from Britain.

The Home Secretary was later not quite sure which happened first, the shouting or the bomb, but suddenly the island of light in the echoing epicentre of the Hall was invaded by a billowing smoke-bomb and shouts of 'Gay is good' and 'Vice is versa' rang around their startled ears. From up the aisles swiftly and smoothly uniformed men appeared, to drag away struggling individuals whilst the cameras swung around and searched for little pockets of activity.

'Oh blast' said Jonathan, for she had withdrawn her hand. The large one turned and stared at him.

'Cecil isn't queer is he?'

'No.'

'I didn't think so either. I can tell.'

'I bet you can,' thought Jonathan.

Within two minutes it was over. Smooth efficiency had

damped the demonstration. The bombs had been removed followed by the kicking, struggling individuals, who
even now were on their way to Notting Hill Police Station
and the tender mercies of Detective Love.

'I shall have them all deported' said the Home Secretary, and the audience laughed. He wasn't joking.

Jonathan felt the body next to him slump down under
the table. 'She's passed out' he thought. 'I wonder what
she's on', and he looked about for some attendants. But
soon he changed his mind. This time he felt her mouth
where her fingers had been. Jonathan suppressed a sigh of
surprise. He leant forward, elbows on the table, while the
Home Secretary droned on. Between his legs below the
table she toyed happily with him, tonguing and lipping.

There was applause from everywhere.

'Ladies and gentlemen,' said the Home Secretary at
length, 'I give you the Prime Minister.'

More applause and even cheers from high above.
Jonathan, finely tongue tickled, came superbly as the PM
rose. The body appeared beside him once again. She
seemed a little sobered by her work.

'You're mad' said Jonathan nicely, tickling her ear with
his tongue.

'Penguins' she said, agreeing.

He leant in close to her and whispered what a judge
would call obscenities in to what a doctor would call her
ear.

'Why not?' she said.

They left the Prime Minister to his dull speech and hand
in hand raced round the circular corridors of the Albert
Hall.

'Where oh where?' said Jonathan.

'Here oh here' said the body pushing him into a little store-room, where she raised her skirts and took him properly like a Christian.

'You're very nice' he said at last.

'Penguins too' she said.

As they walked slowly back around the corridors of Albert's Memorial Hall, they heard a shouting in the lobby: Splendiman was wrestling with a tall red-faced ex-army figure of about eight thousand a year.

'Where is my boy?' said the tall figure far from gently.

'I'm sure the young gentleman in question has come to no harm in particular' said Splendiman loyally.

'Out of my way' said the tall man throwing Splendiman aside.

The large one turned and looked at Jonathan closely as they slid back into their seats. Jonathan beamed her back a smile. She turned away.

'Her Majesty the Queen', said the Prime Minister, 'has decided to take up residence in Australia. Her Majesty's Government have acceded to her request to continue to remain the duly elected government. The constitutional situation will be examined during the next few weeks However, any constitutional changes will only be effected . . . constitutionally.'

Cheers.

'The royal assent will for the moment be held in abeyance. But . . .'

There was a murmur of disapproval from one of the entrances. Somebody evidently was struggling to get in The murmur turned to sounds of alarm as a tall figure broke away from the attendant and advanced towards the stage area. He entered the pool of light and stood for a moment. The Prime Minister stopped speaking and looked glumly at the intruder. Lord Bishop, for it was he indeed, raised an enormous horsewhip.

'Where's my boy?' His voice echoed round the lofty silences of the Hall. Nobody moved.

'Where's my Bobo? What have you done with him?'

The Prime Minister gawped, opening and shutting his mouth like a fish. No sound emerged.

'Where is my boy?'

Crack! The whip snaked out and shook itself with a pistol shot. Lord Bishop took a step forward. The Prime Minister watched him helplessly.

'You are a celebrated pervert', thundered his Lordship, 'and you have corrupted my boy.'

A questioning murmer from the audience. They stirred fascinated.

'I denounce you as a notable pederast and corrupter of youth, and I shall thrash you here before this august assembly.' His Lordship advanced on the little PM raising the great horsewhip menacingly. The PM gulped.

Suddenly, from behind him the Home Secretary, a strange glint in his eyes, leapt to his feet and sprang onto the table. Dramatically he stood between the two protagonists.

'This a job for Captain Marvellous!' the Home Secretary declaimed. He started to remove his clothing – first his jacket, then his shirt and finally his trousers – to reveal (for him) a magnificent silk costume with an enormous 'M' emblazoned on the chest, but in fact (for them) some rather shabby underwear. Lord Bishop paused, astonished at this remarkable intervention; gazed, amazed at the Home Secretary stripped down to his Y-front and vest; could only gawp in turn when this figure pointed straight at him and yelled . . .

'Shazaam!'

Instantly, at the magic word, nothing happened. Lord Bishop did not disappear as Captain Marvellous had half expected, so with one bound he leapt unsteadily to the floor and started grappling with the astounded peer. Uproar in the house.

'To bad I had to reveal my secret identity' said Captain Marvellous in his underpants.

Uniformed attendants came running from everywhere. Even Splendiman appeared, white-faced and shaken. From the very top of the Albert Hall small blackish grey particles started to fall gently like dirty snow. They drifted slowly down into the pool of light and fell upon the wrestling writhing bodies on the Hall floor. They fell upon the Prime Minister, who stood with tears in his eyes, helplessly holding the remains of his speech, watching his lovers's father fighting with the semi-nude Home Secretary.

'I shall deport you' shouted Captain Marvellous, a little out of character.

The black snow fell slowly.

Beside Jonathan, the body whispered as she rose. 'I must make sure that Daddy is alright.'

'Who's Daddy?' said Jonathan.

'The Chancellor' said Lady Candida as she left his side. Slowly it clicked. She, the Chancellor's daughter; he, Jonathan.

'Ten!' yelled Jonathan at the top of his voice. 'I've done it' he shouted into the noise around him. 'Herrington's record is broken. I've had all the daughters of the Cabinet.

every single one!' and he started to beat the table with delight. He began to sing, 'I've had all the daughters of the Ca-binet, I've had all the daughters of the Ca-binet . . .'

'No you haven't' said a chill voice opposite him. Was it . . . the large one? She was looking at him now in a strange way.

'What did you say?'

'You haven't had all the daughters of the Cabinet.'

'Yes I have said Jonathan.

'No you haven't said the large one standing. 'You haven't had me. . . yet.'

'No' said Jonathan shaking his head.

'Yes' said the large one. 'The new Foreign Secretary.'

'Oh no' said Jonathan.

'Well let's just see what you're made of shall we? I think the entertainment's finished here' she said smiling and moving menacingly towards him.

'No, no, I've finished. I've won.'

'You haven't won yet, you political groupie, so let's see what you can do.'

She made a grab at him. Jonathan backed away in his chair and half-rose. 'Now look' he said feebly.

'All right I'll look' said Mrs Pyrrh's enormous little girl, staring at his crotch. 'Now let's just see if you can really win.'

'No, no' said Jonathan, turning to run.

'Yes, yes' said the large one as she panted after him.

The audience were now on their feet. Chaos reigned. Several groups of gay liberators, convinced Lord Bishop was a demonstrator, poured on to the stage to free him. The Home Secretary in his Y-fronts ran around shouting 'Splat! Blam! Take that you finky villain!' reducing the efforts of the uniformed attendants to helpless frustration.

Upon them all the ashes of Cecil's good friend fel[l] steadily and sedately, and in their midst the PM, picke[d] out in the light, stood up on his chair and announced int[o] the microphone: 'I have heard the clarion call. Oh, wh[o] will join me? Brothers and sisters, I shall lead a crusad[e] into the Truce's Noman land!'

'Good man' said the Home Secretary in his underpants 'I knew you weren't a poove. We'll bring back our RAF.'

'Oh sod the RAF,' said the PM, 'it's Bobo we'll b[e] bringing back.'

At the magic sound of Bobo, Lord Bishop seemed to g[o] beserk. The Home Secretary popped him on the chin an[d] he went down amidst a mass of struggling bodies.

'Are you gay?' a demonstrator asked the happy Hom[e] Secretary.

'No, just a little light-hearted' replied the Captain Marvellously.

'Oh dear,' said Jeffrey from backstage, 'I shall be look-ing for a job.'

'Can I help you?' said Lady Candida.

'You know, I think you can' said Jeffrey.

'This country', shouted the PM, his mind ringing with Neville Chamberlain, 'is now at war with Noman's land.'

'That means we are at peace' said someone keen on logic from the audience.

'We shall destroy them' said the small PM, puzzling a million viewers. 'They shall not pass. We will fight them on their beaches, until they give us Bobo back!'

Television zoomed in. It was a great oration. Every word was relayed to ten million startled homes.

'But I thought you loved *me*?' said Splendiman in close

166

up to the PM, as Jonathan dashed past pursued by the enormous one, daughter of the latest Foreign Secretary.

'This is a job for Captain Marvellous!' said the Home Secretary, starting to rip off his clothes, forgetting that he had done so already. 'A shame I must reveal my secret identity' he said, revealing his all as he pulled off his underpants. 'Now do you all recognize me?' he said as he stood there as naked as his bath time, tubby and determined. With one bound (well two), he leapt towards the table where the PM stood and raised his arms aloft to the totally puzzled and outraged audience.

'Whatever shall become of us?' said the Chancellor sadly from his platform seat, while his daughter screwed the PM's Private Secretary backstage.

'You can come home with me if you like' said a little gay voice to him nicely.

'Never fear,' said the Prime Minister as the naked fatty form of the Home Secretary advanced towards him, 'I have the solution. This man shall be Prime Minister!'

'Powee!' said Captain Marvellous, 'PM at last! Kiss me Hardy!' and with that he planted a wild kiss on the PM's lips. Naked he stepped back and surveyed his sudden benefactor. 'But what about you? Will you be my Boy Wonder?'

There was a faraway look in the little PM's eyes. 'It is a far, far better thing' he said, tugging at his clothing, 'that I do now', pulling at his shirt . . .

'Bugger me, they've all gone fucking mad' said the Minister for Pollution.

'Well, be my Home Secretary then?' pleaded the naked Captain Marvellous.

'. . . Than I have ever done before', said the PM finally

stepping out of his trousers to reveal underneath a wonderful green cocktail frock with gathered sleeves and a sensible neckline.

'Be my Chancellor then', exhorted the naked Captain.

'Far far better to have lived and loved badly' declaimed the PM, clipping on a string of evening pearls and stepping into a pair of matching green evening shoes. 'Then never to have loved at all.'

'Well alright, be my Foreign Secretary, then, anything, oh go on, please,' said the Captain, naked in the glare of the television lights.

'No,' said the PM happily, slipping on a fully permed wig. 'Nothing of the sort. I shall be your Queen!'

God Save Our Gracious Queen, struck up the Band on cue, 'Long live our noble Queen' joined in the dumb-struck congregation. 'God save the Queen'.

'Send him victorious . . .
Happy and glorious. . . . '

Suddenly from along the Hallway, the entire Band of the Welsh Guards appeared stark ███ ███ ███ ███ revealed ███ ███ ███ ███ ███ ███. Just how ███ ███ ███ ███ between ███ figures on ███ ███ ███ ███ ███ . , ███ ███ with ███ ███ ; ███ ███ ███ ███ ███ ███ ███ ███ ███ ███ on ███ ███ to ███ and ███ ███ ███ ███

'Well I never' said Jonathan, thoroughly amazed and surprised, 'whoever would have thought it would all end like that.'